Stripper of the Yard

By

Jo Jenner

Jenny Cartwright has worked in the Blue Lagoon Gentleman's Club for sixteen years when overnight her world changes.

Charlie Swansen has a heart attack in the club and dies before he regains consciousness. He leaves £250,000 and some shares to Jenny.

Jenny doesn't realise she has the casting vote in a multi-billion pound buyout, She wants to follow Charlie's wishes but no-one knows what they were.

Jenny and her friends start to fall victim to a number of accidents, it looks like there may be more to the buyout than meets the eye.

Who stands to gain most from Jenny's decision?

Who is the mystery man following Jenny around?

What trouble has Mike gotten himself into?

These and many other questions need to be answered for Jenny to make the right decision and protect her friends.

Stripper of the yard

Chapter one – Happy retirement?

She was already down to her G-string and expertly hanging upside down from one of the two poles on the ends of the T shaped stage, when Charlie rushed into the club. He sat down in his usual chair and smiled at her. He looked different today, happier somehow but she had been hanging upside down a while now and that tended to skew her vision somewhat.

Jenny Cartwright had been a stripper at the Blue Lagoon Gentlemen's Club for the last 16 years. She tended to only work afternoons these days, at thirty-five she was considered too old for the young stag do's

that dominated Friday and Saturday nights. She still had the looks and a fantastically taut body, hanging from poles was one of the best workouts a woman could get, and taking your clothes off for a living meant you never allowed those few pounds to creep on as it could cost you in tips. Jenny was five foot five, with a mane of blonde hair flowing all the way down her back which she utilised in her act to great effect. As the music finished she righted herself and waved at Charlie. She rushed off stage, through the sparkly curtains towards the changing rooms, as the next girl appeared.

Charlie Swansen was one of Jenny's regulars and he had been coming to see her every Wednesday afternoon for years, he didn't even come to see her strip anymore, they were friends and he liked to chat to her. She really took an interest in what he had to say, not like his family, the way he talked, they just seemed to be after what they could get from him. Jenny never took anything from him, though he had to buy her drinks at vastly over inflated prices and vastly watered down ABV, but that was the rule of the club and not Jenny's fault.

'Hi Charlie, how you feeling today?' Jenny emerged from the back wearing lacy underwear and a thin kimono style dressing gown, the uniform of the club when the girls were working but not stripping.

'Good, thanks Jenny. I've made a decision about the company. I am about to become a man of leisure and we are going to celebrate. Let's get some real champagne for a change.' Charlie was smiling from ear to ear.

'Wow real champagne, you know how much that costs in here?'

'I don't care, today is a day for good news and celebrating. Mike bring us some real champagne, and you can open it over here. If I'm paying your prices I want to see the bottle.' Charlie shouted over to the club's owner and head barman.

Mike was an ex bouncer with a heart of gold who had taken over the club ten years before. He brought in a couple of the girls off the streets and helped them get clean of drugs, but he was careful with money. Since a lot of the new fancy clubs set up, the Blue Lagoon Gentlemen's Club started losing clients. Mike now manned the bar during the day. It saved him money on bar staff and bouncers. The girls worked as waitresses when not stripping or entertaining clients, so Mike could easily manage the bar on his own. The Blue Lagoon Gentlemen's Club was strangely named as the whole interior was bright red, or had been bright red; it was now more dull scarlet.

Mike appeared from behind the bar carrying bottle of champagne in an ice bucket in one hand and two glasses in the other. He wound his way through the tables set up facing the stage towards Charlie and Jenny, sat in one of the booths that ran along the back wall of the club. With Charlie paying such an over inflated price for his champagne Mike wasn't about to insist he paid for a

private dance. It wasn't as if there were hoards of

customers waiting to use the booths. The club was in Hurt's Yard in the centre of Nottingham and shared its location with an eclectic mix of junk shops, specialist shops and clubs. The Blue Lagoon was helped by this association in the 1980's when it was a thriving part of town. Now The Yard was used more as a cut through for shoppers and tended not to be spotted by those touring the town on a drunken night out. Mike made his money on expensive drinks and private dances but the big money was made from stag dos. These days the best stag dos paid to get into the expensive clubs with the best girls, the Blue Lagoon tended more towards council estate and this had led to even Mike having to hire extra bouncers, as the lads could sometimes get a little carried away.

'There you go Charlie, the best in the house.' The cork popped and Mike quickly filled the glasses with Moet. 'Whatcha celebrating?'

'Hopefully retirement.'

'Retirement, surely not. You're only young.'

'Come on Mike I'm sixty, over-weight, balding and unfit. I have problems catching my breath just walking from the car to the office. I think it's time to rest up a little.'

'Rest up? I can't imagine you pottering around the garden somehow.'

'Oh no, I'm going to write my memoirs. You wouldn't believe how much corruption and back stabbing there is in the pharmaceutical business. It'll be quite an eye opener.'

'Well you enjoy yourself, and hopefully you'll still have time to pop down and see Jenny.'

'Oh yes,' Charlie smiled at Jenny. 'I wouldn't miss that for the world.'

Mike wandered off and Jenny looked closely at Charlie. He did look tired today, more so than usual and he was sweating. It was warm in the club, to stop the girls complaining that they had to walk round with nothing on, but it wasn't hot.

'Are you okay? You don't look so good.' Jenny held her hand to Charlie's brow. He was burning up.

'Yes I'm fine. I'm not going to let a little touch of the flu spoil my day.' Charlie ran a finger round the edge of his collar and loosened his tie. 'Let's enjoy this fine champagne.'

Charlie lifted his glass and chinked it against Jenny's. He gulped the drink down and quickly poured himself another.

'Charlie. You sure you're all right?'

He was really starting to sweat and he undid the top button of his shirt. Jenny had never seen him look anything other than immaculate.

'Let me get you some water.' She waved at Mike and he rushed over, seeing the look of concern on her face.

'What's up?'

'It's Charlie. I don't think he feels too good. Can we get him some water?'

'Yeh sure, why don't you take him through to the office, it's a bit cooler in there.' Mike could see Charlie looked ill and he definitely didn't need a customer collapsing in the middle of the club.

'Come on Charlie,' Jenny helped him up but he was disorientated, and struggled to stand on his own.

'I'm fine, no need to worry.' Charlie was slurring his words and slumped against her. He looked like he'd had two bottles of champagne, not two glasses.

Jenny struggled to get him to the office and laid him on the couch just as Mike returned with the water. She managed to get him to drink a little, but he was slipping in and out of consciousness.

'Mike we need to call an ambulance.' Jenny knew he didn't want to bring attention to the club but Charlie needed help.

'Isn't Carly in today?' Mike asked.

'Yeh. She should be in by now.'

'Okay, you go and fetch her, I'll stay here. I'm sure he's fine, just the flu.'

Jenny rushed off to the girls' changing room and ran straight into Carly just as she was coming through the back door, weighed down by medical journals.

'Whoa! Jenny, what's the rush?' She smiled.

'Quick Carly. It's Charlie! He's collapsed and Mike

won't let me call an ambulance, I need you to look at

him.'

'Okay, where is he?' Carly dropped her books onto the

dressing table and rushed after Jenny.

Jenny and Carly ran into the office just as Mike was

hanging up Charlie's jacket.

'He woke up and was too hot so I took his jacket off.

He's unconscious again.' Mike explained as the two girls

rushed passed him to Charlie's side.

Carly felt for a pulse and turned to Mike.

'He's very weak Mike. We need to call an ambulance

and we need to do it now.'

'But the club… I can't have ambulance crews traipsing

through here.'

'Well if you don't get them here soon you'll have the

police 'cause he'll be dead.'

'Ambulance please.' Whilst they'd been arguing, Jenny

had been on the phone.

'They're on their way.' She looked at Mike and dared

him to question her.

Chapter two – Mrs Swansen I presume

Jenny sat in the waiting room of the Queen's Medical Centre waiting to hear about Charlie. She looked around her wondering what tragedies brought all these people into A&E on a Wednesday afternoon. TV programmes make you believe that A&E is always full of drunks but, here now it was full of everyday people; most seemed to have children with them. Her palms were sweating. She just needed to check Charlie was okay and then she could leave.

'Coffee?' Carly handed her a khaki brown plastic cup containing a similarly coloured insipid looking liquid. The only thing you could say about the coffee was that it was hot. What material the cup was made out of, to contain a liquid of such temperature is known only to the makers of vending machines across the world.

'Thanks. Have you found anything out?'

Charlie had been unconscious for the whole of the ambulance journey and once they arrived at the hospital they had been left in A&E reception while the important business of checking on Charlie was taking place. They left for a few minutes while Carly organised a change of clothes for Jenny but other than that they had not moved.

'He's being assessed now, but it sounds like a heart attack. I think they may have to operate. The student doctor is on the same placement as me so he says he will let us know once Charlie's been checked over.'

'Thanks for this Carly,' Jenny squeezed her hand.

'Are you okay? You look like you've seen a ghost and your hand, it's all clammy. Wait there, I'm getting some help.'

'No Carly, it's okay. I just don't like hospitals.'

'No way. You're burning up. That's not a fear of hospitals. You might have whatever Charlie's got.'

'If you stop panicking and sit down, I'll tell you something I've never told the other girls, but you must promise to calm down.'

Carly sat down and held her friend's hand.

'I can still remember it like it was yesterday,' Jenny began. 'I was staying in foster care with my daughter.'

'You have a daughter? Why have we never met her?'

'If you'll let me finish.' Jenny was beginning to regret her decision to confide in Carly.

'Sorry, go on,'

'Her name was Mary and she was a beautiful baby. She had always been a good sleeper but I woke up one night and the room felt unnaturally silent. I crept over to the cot to make sure she was okay. She usually slept well but if she woke she had lungs good enough to wake the whole street. As I stood over the cot I still couldn't hear her breathing and when I touched her she was cold. So cold. The rest of that night is a blur. I can remember Dave and Emma, my foster parents, rushing in and calling the ambulance and the panicked trip to the hospital. Then all I remember is the look on the doctor's face as he told me that Mary was dead. I will never forget that look. I've tried not to visit hospitals since then, but when I do it brings back such bad memories.'

'Oh Jenny, I am so sorry.' Carly slung her arms around her friend and gave her a huge hug.

'She would have been about your age now and I always wonder how she would have turned out.'

Jenny sipped her coffee feeling slightly less panicked than before. She was glad she had told Carly and knew her friend would be watching out for her. She decided to try and read one of the many out of date magazines to take her mind off her surroundings. Within minutes she gave up and started paying more attention to the varied groups of people waiting to be seen. Wondering what their stories could have been.

Jenny's attention, along with most other people in reception, was drawn to a glamorous woman who pushed herself to the front of the queue at the reception desk.

'Excuse me, excuse me,' she must have been in her early twenties, looked about six feet tall, mainly due to the five inch heels she wore, and most of her was plastic. If it wasn't for the fact she was brunette, Jenny could have sworn a real-life Barbie doll had just walked into the hospital. She was wearing a tight navy blue dress which hugged her in all the right places and was short enough to catch people's attention, but not so short as to be trashy. She was definitely the modern Essex girl in action.

'My husband is here. I need to see him straight away.' The receptionist was obviously trying to ignore her and deal with people in the correct order, but the rest of the queue had moved aside. This was a woman used to getting her own way.

'Can I help you, err Madam?' The receptionist raised an eyebrow.

'Yes, I need to see my husband right away.'

'And his name?'

'Swansen, Charlie Swansen.'

Jenny's jaw dropped as she turned to Carly.

'That's Charlie's wife!' He had always come across as so grounded and a real sweetie. Never would Jenny have thought he would have a trophy wife. Didn't only very rich men have trophy wives?

'Mrs Swansen, please come with me,' a distinguished looking man with salt and pepper hair wearing a white coat took the woman's arm and led her towards a door to the side of the reception.

'Just wait a minute,' called a grey-haired Wallis Simpson look alike who had just entered the building. 'I need to come with you too.'

'And who are you?' The doctor asked.

'I'm Charlie's wife.'

'No, you're not-' shouted the younger woman. 'He left you a long time ago. He needs me now.'

'Strange. He told me last week you weren't the woman he thought you were when he married you.'

The younger woman thrust out her hand and slapped Wallis. The doctor managed to part them and Jenny ran over to try and help.

Once things calmed down and the doctor established the current Mrs Swansen was Marissa, the younger woman, she was led off to see her husband.

The Wallis look alike sat down and Jenny went to fetch her a coffee.

'Thanks for that.' the older woman smiled as Jenny handed her the coffee.

'You might not say that once you've tasted it.'

'You must be Jenny.'

How on earth could this woman know who she was?

'I'm Veronica Smythe, Charlie's first wife. He's told me a lot about you.'

'Really? And how do you feel about me?' Jenny wasn't sure how to take this revelation.

'Oh don't worry. Charlie and I are the best of friends. Even after he left me for that trollop! Not the trollop that's just gone in there but the first trollop. Marissa is the most recent in a long line of younger models, but she was the only one who was sly enough to get him to marry her.'

'I can't believe Charlie is married to someone like that. He always used to sit and chat to me, but he never came across as anything other than a lovely man.'

'Oh, he is. I think he thought for all his wealth he should have a wife that looked like that. He found out too late how much companionship, having someone with at least some intelligence and who was interested in more than just reality TV and the latest fashions, was worth.'

'You don't sound bitter that he left you.' Jenny was very impressed with Veronica. She was very classy looking, wearing a suit that was obviously Chanel, and carried herself with a huge amount of dignity.

'I was at first but life goes on. We had 20 wonderful years together, and we have a fantastic daughter, Vicki. Also I met and married a wonderful man and Charlie got stuck with women like that. I always felt a little sorry for him.'

The doctor steadily walked back into reception smiling at Veronica. 'I have spoken to Mrs Swansen and as Mr Swansen is currently stable, she said it is okay for you to go and see him.'

'Why don't you come too dear?' Veronica asked Jenny and held out her hand.

Jenny looked over at Carly.

'Will you be okay?' Carly said.

19

'I think I'll be fine now. Thanks for staying with me.'

'No probs. I'll see you later but you call if you need

anything.'

Carly gave Jenny another one of her big hugs and
headed out of the hospital. Jenny and Veronica followed
the doctor towards Charlie's private room.

Marissa was sitting by the side of the bed holding
Charlie's hand. She had her head bent and the way her
shoulders were moving she must have been crying. She
glanced up and Jenny noticed there was not a single tear
on her face. The Botox made it hard to judge Marissa's

emotions, but the lack of tears told Jenny everything she
needed to know.

'Can you give us any details doctor?' Veronica asked,
trying to stay calm.

'Well, he has had a massive heart attack. His state of
health through the night is crucial. He is currently
stable, but we need to monitor him closely. I can give
you ladies ten minutes and then I am afraid you will
have to leave.'

The doctor left the room and Marissa looked at Jenny.

'Who are you? The doctor said you brought Charlie in.'

'Yes that's right. I am one of the secretaries from the
office.' Jenny looked over at Veronica and saw her nod

sagely. There was no point upsetting Marissa more than they had to at this stage. 'He collapsed and my friend is a student doctor so we knew to get him to the hospital quickly.'

'Thank you.' Even though the tears weren't flowing she did sound genuinely upset.

The gentle blip, blip of the life support machine that had been ignored in the background turned into a wailing siren. They all jumped and looked at one another, not sure what to do. Jenny rushed over to the door just as a large nurse rushed in. The nurse pushed Jenny out of the way and stood at the end of the bed, quickly taking in the scene around her. She pushed passed Veronica to reach the head of the bed.

'He's crashed, call the team.' The nurse shouted as she pushed an alarm and started moving pillows and bed clothes. The women were pushed out of the room. Even through the window all they could see was a wall of blue scrub wearing medical bodies doing their best to save him.

Chapter three – Suspicions aroused

Charlie never regained consciousness. Before Jenny
left, Veronica promised to let her know about the
funeral. She wanted to say goodbye to Charlie
properly.

Jenny arrived back at the flat to find the lift out of order
yet again. She trudged up the ten flights of stairs
desperate to just get home and shut out the world. As
she finally made it to her floor, Mrs Johnstone was
coming out of the flat next door.

'Morning Jenny. Busy day?'

Jenny gave a half smile, 'hospital all afternoon. A friend
of mine died.'

'Oh you poor girl. Come on in, I'll get you a coffee.'

'Thanks Mrs Johnstone, but I just wanted to get in and
go to bed.'

'I understand sweetie. Let me know if you need
anything.'

'Well there is one thing.' Jenny felt bad asking a favour,
but she was exhausted.

'Anything dear.'

'Can you get Mrs Arkwright's shopping? I have a list and the money.'

'Of course, honey.'

Jenny took a long hot bath and went to bed. Two hours of tossing and turning later, she gave up. Making herself a coffee, she sat in the lounge and stared out of the window. How could you be so lonely in the centre of a city? Jenny had lived in the same flat in the Victoria Centre block for fifteen years. It was a dingy flat she rented when she first left her foster home and got a job, and it had been all she could afford. She could have afforded better now, but she was saving up to buy her own club one day and the flat was big enough just for her. It suited her needs for now. For the uninitiated, the block looked very inner city and the place you expected people to go to buy and use drugs. That did happen, but the majority of people who lived in the block were good honest people trying to get by on what little they had. The doorbell rang and Jenny slowly rose from her chair. She didn't want to see anyone right now, but it might be important. As she opened the door, her three best friends threw their arms around her and she knew they were going to make sure she was okay.

Carly had rounded up Blossom and Mindy. Mindy was carrying a carrier bag full of biscuits, tea bags, milk and sugar, Blossom a bottle of wine and Carly a very big box of chocolates. Once Jenny could disengage herself from the hug she walked back into the living room and sat down.

'Wine,' called Blossom from the kitchen.

'No she needs a sweet tea, she's in shock.' Mindy's voice trailed in from the kitchen.

'How you holding up sweetheart?' Carly smiled and sat down next to her on the sofa.

'Not too bad I just can't believe he's gone. I mean he did look ill today, but he said he had a touch of flu.' Jenny stuttered and started to cry. Carly held her tightly. Jenny looked up just as Blossom and Mindy struggled to get through the living room door at the same time and couldn't help but laugh at the sight. Blossom was six feet tall and the skinniest, blackest woman you would ever see, while Mindy nearly a foot shorter and a very pale skinned Asian with the most amazing green eyes. Jenny looked around at her three best friends and knew she could always rely on them. Carly was the last to join the group but she really gelled with the other girls. She never mentioned her background which was so different from the other three. Blossom was 24 years old and lucky to be alive. She had fallen into prostitution and become a heavy drug user to numb the pain. Mike Peters won her in the same poker game he gained the club in, and helped her get clean. He hadn't realised at the time there was a real call for tall, skinny black girls in the strip club world. Mindy was only eighteen years old but had been married to some distant cousin as soon as she turned sixteen. He thought it was a good idea to beat her to show his masculinity, she managed to make a break for it when he hurt her so badly she was hospitalised for more than a week. Her family put more importance on the honour of the marriage and had not spoken to her since, instead accepting her husband's version of events and even letting him stay in their home. Stripping was the only work she managed to get but the Asian clientele at the club was huge, and while the men were very strict with their own wives they still liked to watch Mindy. One of the best shows Mike had was when Mindy and Blossom went on together. It pandered to every stereotype the club members had. Jenny accepted a cup of tea and a glass of wine, precariously balancing both as she tried to get a chocolate.

'I can't believe Charlie was married to Marissa.' Jenny sighed once the girls got her to talk more about Charlie. 'I always thought he was just a sweet old man. But he wasn't really that old. He was only sixty and that is no age to die.'

'She was an amazing looking woman,' grinned Carly. 'Maybe Mike will offer her some work if Charlie has left her destitute!'

'Sounds pretty impressive.' winked Blossom.

'Not your type Blossom,' chuckled Jenny. 'Far too high maintenance.'

'And that Veronica looked like she had enough money not to be worrying about any legacy,' said Carly.

'Well apparently she married again after Charlie left her, so perhaps her second husband had money,' said Jenny.

'There's only one thing that's been worrying me since Charlie died,' Carly looked seriously at Jenny

'What?' the three women turned and stared at Carly.

'Well, it's Charlie's symptoms, they just didn't seem right for a heart attack.'

'How do you mean?' Mindy loved a good scandal.

'He was sweaty and Jenny said he was out of breath and thirsty.' Carly explained.

'Yes but he'd rushed over to the club. He was worried he would be late,' said Jenny

'I know and at Charlie's age with his weight, it could have brought on a heart attack and didn't he say he was suffering from flu for the last few days?'

'Yes. I think it was just Charlie not realising how sick he was. You said it yourself. He was overweight and you know he could sit and drink all afternoon and not look like he'd touched a drop. I know Mike waters down the beer but Charlie loved his whiskey and Mike didn't dare water that down with the prices he was charging. '

'I just think something smells fishy, that's all.' Carly shrugged.

'Anyway what else could it be? You're not trying to suggest foul play are you?' Mindy loved to over dramatize.

'Dah Dah Daaah,' giggled Blossom who had managed to work her way down most of the bottle of wine she had bought to share with Jenny.

'Don't be silly. Who would want to hurt Charlie? He was just a normal bloke who worked in the offices out on Parliament Street. Nothing special.' Jenny turned and flicked the telly on so they could watch The Apprentice together, just a normal Wednesday night. As she did so she looked over at Carly and was disturbed to see the look on her face. She obviously thought there was more to this.

Chapter four – The funeral

The funeral was held a week after Charlie died and
Veronica, as promised, had called Jenny to let her
know. Jenny dug out her court suit and Carly the suit
she wore when she sat in with GP's to view patients and
off they went.

The funeral service was held at St Giles Church in West
Bridgford and Jenny and Carly arrived just as the hearse
was pulling up. The joys of the Nottingham public
transport service had very nearly made them late and
they had to run the last two hundred yards. As the coffin
was taken from the hearse, three other funeral cars
pulled up behind. Marissa emerged from the first car
wearing a dress that was too short and too tight to show
any real respect. The veil she wore made it impossible
to see her face. Jenny suspected this wasn't to hide

make-up smeared with tears. She put a handkerchief
inside the veil every few seconds so maybe she really
was upset. The saddest thing was she was alone; no-one
was there to hold her hand, no-one to give her comfort.
The car behind held Veronica and a woman about
Jenny's age whom she didn't recognise. Veronica was
wearing a mid calf length black dress and a long fur
coat, wrapped up against the cold. No hat, but she
looked drawn, as if she had not slept since the last time
Jenny had seen her. The younger woman with her was

tall and wearing heels. She wore a smart grey trouser
suit that had obviously been made to measure and her
hair was tied up in a chignon. She towered over
Veronica and put a protective hand on her arm as they
stood beside the car. Perfectly made up and postured but
underneath it she looked like she was struggling to hold
it together. The sort of woman who thought it was a
sign of weakness to cry in front of strangers. She had a
presence about her that meant you wouldn't argue with
her unless you were ready for a fight.

The third car contained Terry St John; he was Charlie's
business partner and had been to the club once or twice
when Charlie had taken clients in the early days. He
stood much taller than everyone else and if Jenny
remembered rightly he was a few years younger than
Charlie but looked so different. A full head of hair,
slightly greying at the temples, and not a ounce of fat on
him, Terry had been a champion skier in his youth and
still followed a strict diet and exercise regime even
though he worked fourteen hours days at the company,
he had run with Charlie for the last twenty years.

The coffin was carried into the church and after the
main funeral party had entered everyone else followed.
Jenny and Carly couldn't believe the number of people
who had come to pay their respects. The church, which
held over three hundred people, was full. The vicar

looked as though he wanted to lock all the doors so he could keep them all there until Sunday. The service lasted about an hour and then the coffin was transported to the crematorium. Jenny and Carly had decided not to go to the crematorium and were just starting to leave when they were approached by Terry St John.

'Ladies, do you have a moment?' Terry smiled and started to lead Jenny off to one side, Carly followed.

'Yes of course.' Jenny responded. 'You were Charlie's business partner weren't you?'

'That's right, you have a good memory. It must be fifteen years since we last met, and then only two or three times.'

'I'm good with faces but unfortunately not names.'

'Oh I'm sorry, I'm Terry St John and you're Jenny but I don't think I know your friend.'

'This is Carly; she's here for moral support.'

Terry shook Carly's hand and turned back to Jenny.

'Are you going to the crematorium?'

'Unfortunately as we are reliant on public transport I think by the time we get there everything will be over.'

'That's no problems let me take you both with me.'

'Are you sure? After all we're not family or anything.'

'Well I know Charlie was very fond of you and Veronica said you were a great help at the hospital.'

'That's very nice but I am not sure we should intrude on the family's grief. And Marissa thinks I'm just a secretary. Will it not look odd?'

'That's very sweet of you to be concerned but I do have an ulterior motive. I am the executor of the will and we were hoping to have the reading after the funeral and it would help to have all the beneficiaries there.'

'I'm sure it would but why do you need us?' Jenny asked.

'You are in the will.'

'I am?' Jenny couldn't believe Charlie would have thought to include her in his will. He really was such a sweetie.

'Yes. So you see it would be no inconvenience for me to drive you to the crematorium, then you could come to the wake and listen to the reading of the will. It will make it easier for the rest of the family as once today is over they can start to move forward.'

'Well… thank you very much. We really appreciate it.'

The service was very brief and quiet compared to the church. Not many people had made the journey even though it was less than three miles. It felt more like the final farewell for the family. The church service had been for everyone who knew him and the crematorium was just for the close few. Jenny felt like she was intruding and sat at the back with Carly. When the family left she was sure Marissa gave her a funny look, as if to say why were Charlie's secretary and a doctor from the hospital at Charlie's funeral but Marissa's veil was so thick when she mentioned it to Carly, she just told her she was being paranoid.

The wake was held in Charlie's house out on the road to Ruddington. The house stood alone on a hill and Jenny remembered her Gran had called it Southfork after the house in Dallas when it was first built. It had the look of an old fashioned manor house with the red bricks of a property built in the eighties. There was a circular driveway that was not hidden from the main road so all the fancy cars parked outside could be seen by passersby, and the helipad was ostentatious even if no-one had ever seen it being used. The wake was similar to most wakes with little sandwiches and glasses of sherry with the exception being there were servants serving them rather than the widow or a member of the family. Jenny and Carly stood in the doorway of a drawing room that was bigger than the whole of Jenny's flat, wondering why they were there and what they should do. Veronica spotted them and made her way over.

'Aaah Jenny, glad you could make it' She smiled; she had a way of making you feel comfortable but knowing that you were definitely not in the same class.

'Thank you for inviting me. This is my friend Carly. I hope you don't mind us coming up to the house but Mr St John asked us to.'

'Oh no that's fine, help yourselves to some food and wine,' she signalled to a waiter who came over with a tray of glasses of sherry and was quickly followed by a waitress with a tray of hors d'oeuvres.

'How have you been?' Jenny asked. 'It must have been tough on you this week.'

'Oh thank you for asking, dear. Unfortunately Marissa thinks the job of a widow is to lock herself in her room and be inconsolable, so all this has been left to me. Luckily Vicki is a tower of strength and has helped massively.'

'Vicki?'

'Of course, you've never met. Vicki darling, can you come here please?' Veronica called over the woman in the grey suit who had been with her at the funeral.

'Vicki this is Jenny and Carly. Jenny was your father's friend I mentioned. We met at the hospital. Jenny, Carly this is Vicki. Mine and Charlie's daughter.'

'Ah yes I remember. Mother told me about you. Marissa is going to love you being here.' Vicki shook hands with the two visitors and grinned.

'I am so sorry about your father.' Carly said. 'Did he have a history of heart disease?'

'No, that's the strange thing, even though he was overweight, he had a medical just three weeks ago and they had said he was fighting fit.'

Vicki looked like she wanted to say more, but she and her mother were called away to talk to another guest.

'What are you playing at?' Jenny whispered to Carly.

'Well I still think there's something fishy going on, and there is obviously no love lost between the first Mrs Swansen and her daughter and the current Mrs Swansen is there?'

'Just because they don't like each other doesn't mean foul play.'

'Well I don't like it.'

A tall young man in a business suit wandered over, 'Hi there. I'm Cecil Moreau, Charlie's assistant at CVV publishing I don't think we've been introduced.'

'I'm Jenny and this is Carly. We're old friends of

Charlie's. I thought Charlie ran a pharmaceutical

company.'

'CVV publishing was just a hobby really. Charlie set it

up for Vicki but she only wanted to work for the big

pharmaceutical firm, so most of the publishing work

was left to me. It's been running five years now and

really starting to show a profit.'

'Why didn't Vicki want to work in publishing?'

'Not sure she even knew that's why Charlie set it up, to

tell you the truth. Not great communicators the

Swansens.'

Terry St John tapped his fork against his crystal

whiskey glass, 'Ladies and Gentlemen, I think we have

everyone here who is included in the will so if you don't

mind, can we make our way through to the dining room

where the solicitor is waiting to read it.'

A butler threw open the double doors at the end of the

drawing room and six people walked through and took

their seats. Terry asked Carly if she wouldn't mind

staying in the drawing room. As Jenny wandered

through the huge double doors she wondered how the Charlie she had known could have lived in a place like this. She had always though he was just an average Joe. Well off but hardly Alan Sugar.

The people round the dining table all focused on the solicitor. Jenny tried to size them up. To the solicitors left, a couple who looked like the faithful retainers always seen on the TV in murder mysteries, next to them was Cecil Moreau, then Terry St John, Veronica and Vicki, then Jenny, and to her right, Marissa.
The solicitor started to read the will and Jenny continued to look around. Veronica was the only one who looked unconcerned, she must have enough money to not need anything Charlie could leave her, thought Jenny. The old couple looked like anything would be a treat to them. They sat very close together and the wife would dab her eyes with her handkerchief every so often. The husband placed his arm around her and with his other hand held her's. The only one she couldn't

work out was Cecil; he was a normal employee so why would he be here?
The solicitor had finally gotten to the bit about who had been left what.
'To Mr and Mrs Jenkins who have tended the house and garden for me wherever I have lived I leave them the

cottage in Ruddington they currently rent and £100,000 to see them into their old age.'

Mr and Mrs Jenkins were grinning and hugging each other, but no-one else seemed phased that they had been left so much money. How much was Charlie worth?

'To Cecil Moreau I leave CVV publishing on the understanding he may not change the name.' Cecil smiled to himself and rubbed his hands together.

'To my friend and the person who always listened no matter how boring I was, Jenny, I leave 14% of my shares in Pharmcorp, and trust that she will know what to do for the best. I also leave her £250,000 so she can set up on her own and get out of that terrible flat.

The room all turned and stared at Jenny. She assumed this was due to the large amount of money, not knowing anything about shares.

'To Veronica, my friend, my confident and the mother of my child, I leave the portrait collection and my mother's jewellery she has always so much admired.'

'That must be worth a couple of million.' Marissa burst out. 'I knew you were just trying to get something out of this.'

Veronica looked at Marissa as if she was a spoilt child.

'I leave to Vicki, my wonderful capable daughter, the rest of my shares in Pharmcorp and the house in St Lucia she loves to visit.

'To my wonderful wife I leave the tenure of Homestead for her life and it will then revert to Vicki upon Marissa's death. I also leave Marissa a trust which will give her an allowance of £10,000 a month until her death.'

'£10,000 what am I supposed to do with that,' Marissa screamed. 'That's not even going to keep me in dresses. I thought you loved me Charlie,' she called as her eyes looked to the ceiling and she rushed out of the room.

At this everyone started talking at once and all of them ignored Jenny.

Jenny slowly rose and went to find Carly. She was in shock. £250,000. She couldn't believe it. After she found Carly, they asked the butler to call them a cab, and he went to fetch the chauffeur to drive them back into town. Terry St John opened the dining room door slightly and crept out, the noise of arguments could be heard inside.

'Jenny, please take my card and get in touch early next week so we can sort this out.'

Jenny looked at him blankly.

'Well firstly we need to transfer the money over to you and you need to attend the board meeting.'

'I am sure the board doesn't want me there.' she smiled.

'Jenny I don't think you understand. With 14% of Charlie's shares, you have a 7% stake in a three billion pound business. More importantly, the way the other shares are split you could have the casting vote. So it's irrelevant whether the board wants you there or not. They need you there. Anyway I need to get back.' Terry handed her his card and crept back into the dining room as the butler appeared with their coats.

Chapter five – Decisions, decisions.

Once Jenny got home the vast amount of money she had been left started to sink in. She looked around her flat. Was it really so bad? Charlie had wanted her to move out but he didn't realise how safe she felt there. The community was something she had never had before and she didn't want to give it up yet. What she did want to give up was stripping. She loved the club and her friends but being ogled by drunken men was not her idea of the most wonderful job in the world. It had got her off the streets, meant she had made some great friends and been able to help people, but now was the time to look into getting her own club. She was getting too old to be balancing upside down. It was time to talk to Mike and let him know she was leaving.

Jenny arrived at the club early on Thursday morning just as Mike was restocking the bar.

'Morning Mike fancy a coffee,' she called as she wandered through.

'Yes please I'd love one.'

Jenny reappeared moments later and sat at the end of the bar. Mike was the only man, other than Charlie, Jenny had ever trusted and she didn't want to let him down, but she needed to move on. Before she had chance to explain everything to Mike, he started shedding his troubles.

'I don't think I can keep this up much longer Jenny,' he said looking tired. Jenny hadn't noticed before. Mike always seemed so strong, how could she have missed the signs?

'What's wrong Mike, you look exhausted?'

'The club's not been making money for the last few months and I don't think I can go on with it much longer. I owe money and there seems to be fewer punters every week.'

'Have you thought about revamping it? You know advertising, special offers, special theme nights. I was even thinking you could put on some male strippers and get some hen parties in.' Jenny said.

'Wow Jenny you've really been thinking. I wish I'd have known, we could have tried something, but you know my hearts just not in it anymore. The only thing stopping me from closing it down right now is the girls. I know you'll be alright, but people like Mindy and Blossom they've got nowhere else to go and I don't want to let them down.'

'I don't know how to say this Mike but Charlie left me some money and I was coming in this morning to let you know I was leaving.'

'Well that's it; I may as well close now.' Mike wiped his hand on a bar towel and sat down heavily.

'If you'll let me finish, I was going to say I am looking to leave and buy my own club, so why don't I buy this one?'

'Oh Jenny! I do love you,' Mike laughed. 'But you can't afford to pay me what I need to cover my debts and leave me with both my legs intact.'

'I think I can. Charlie left me two hundred and fifty thousand pounds in his will.'

'How much?' Mike whistled. 'He must have really had a soft spot for you.'

'It seems Charlie was worth a lot more than we ever thought.'

'Jenny the club has been losing money for months and I owe some nasty people. I can't let you get involved in this.'

'Let me be the judge of that. How much do you need?'

Mike bowed his head and muttered into the counter, 'fifty grand should get the loan sharks and the brewery off my back but I'm not sure how we can turn this place round. There's no point you wasting the money Charlie gave you.'

'I told you we can revamp it. Give those clubs up in the Lace Market a run for their money.'

Mike smiled and grabbed Jenny's hand, giving it a massive squeeze. 'You don't know what this means to me. Don't worry I will be out of your hair as soon as I am sure the loan sharks have cleared out.'

'Don't be silly I need you to help me run the club. If that's okay?'

'Jenny you have to be the most amazing person ever.'

'Good, let's have some of you real champagne to celebrate the deal and then this afternoon I need to get over to Charlie's solicitors to sign some forms and find out about these shares.'

Jenny was still sat at the end of the bar as a young man in his early twenties came in the club and started to have a go at Mike. He was average height and build but had a cocky self assured manner. Mike quickly bundled the man out of the main club, but instead of throwing him into the street he took him into the office.

Jenny finished her drink and was heading back to the dressing room to collect some of her personal items just as the man left the office.

'And don't forget we need this sorting out,' the young man called into the office. As he was walking away he glanced at Jenny and quickly looked away trying to hide his face.

Mike left the office and as Jenny looked at him, he shook his head and walked off back towards the bar.

Jenny arrived at the solicitor's office to sort out the money and the shares.

'Ah Miss Cartwright, nice to see you again.' Mr McGuffin the solicitor shook Jenny's hand as she entered his office. Jenny concentrated hard but couldn't remember ever having met the man before. 'I read the will.'

'Of course you did. So sorry it's just everything about that day is a little blurred.'

'That's quite all right. A lot of people don't recognise me after those things. I suppose the last thing on your mind is remembering what the solicitor looks like.'

Jenny smiled and accepted a cup of tea and settled down to try to understand what she was entitled to.

'Now the family are contesting the shares that have been left to you but I am trying to talk them into not going to probate,' said Mr McGuffin.

'Well the shares mean nothing to me, so they can have them if it helps.'

'Don't be so eager to give up what Charlie wanted you to have. I have a letter here to you from Charlie which the will instructed me to give to you away from everyone else.'

Jenny took the letter and started to read.

My darling Jenny,

I hope you understand how much you have meant to me over the years. I have never had to pretend to be who I'm not with you and you have never judged me or wanted anything from me. That has meant the world to me. I hope you understand I could not leave you more as etiquette dictates I must look after my family, no

45

matter how often they have disappointed me or let me
down. I hope the money will be enough to get you out of
the god forsaken hole you live in.
The most important thing I have left you is some of my
shares. Leaving you 14% of my shares means you have
a 7% stake in the company. At the moment there are
moves afoot to sell the company and I have not yet
decided if it is the best thing for the company and for
the workers but I do know it will be the best thing for
the share holders. I want you to look at the offer and
make sure the staff is going to be okay. If you decided
we should sell then you shares will be worth about two
hundred million pounds. I know I can trust you to do the
right thing as you are the most honest person I have
ever met.
Make me proud.
Charlie.

Jenny looked back at the solicitor too shocked to speak.
She raised her cup of tea to her lips but her hands were
shaking so much she had to put it down again. She took
a couple of deep breaths and tried to drink her tea again.
The cup was still shaking slightly but she was much
more in control than before. After sipping her tea and
reading the letter through again. She looked at Mr
McGuffin. 'I don't think I can do what Charlie is asking

me to do. How can he expect me to make sure the staff is okay?'

'Turns out Charlie was right about you,' Mr McGuffin chuckled

'How do you mean?'

'Well you've just been told your worth over two hundred million pounds and your first concern is the staff. Charlie chose well'

'How can my shares be worth so much?'

'The company will be worth three billion pounds if this sale goes ahead and you own 7%.'

'How can anything be worth so much? I don't think I would know what to do with that sort of money. What happens if the company isn't sold?'

'Well everything should continue as before. The company won't grow without a cash investment from someone, but your shares will not become worthless.' Mr McGuffin. 'I can see this is an awful lot for you to take in. Is there anything I can do to help?'

'Well I need to understand all the implications before I make any kind of decision.'

'Charlie knew you wouldn't be swayed by the money. He just wanted someone with your morals to check the rest of them weren't doing anything dodgy.'

'Wait a minute, on the day Charlie died he said he was celebrating his retirement so he must have decided to sell,' Jenny breathed a sigh of relief.

'Not necessarily. He was getting ready to retire and he wanted to make the decision on this deal before he did. He must have decided which way to go. Did he not tell you?'

'No. Damn. I still have no idea what to do. Well I shall try my best but what if the family stops me from getting the shares.'

'There is a board meeting at the end of the month where the sale will be discussed and if the shares have not been allocated, the meeting and the sale can't go ahead. I shall urge them to settle the will on the basis you will not know what you are doing. If I talk to them separately I can convince them you will vote the way each of them wants you to and that should ensure the will goes through. I have been Charlie's solicitor for the

last forty years and if he wanted you to have these shares I will do everything I can to make sure you get them. '

'Okay, and in the meantime I think I need to talk to some experts about this deal.'

'Yes please do. There is a lot on the internet but there is also lots of paperwork I can get you to read. Now it there anything else you need?'

'I don't really like to ask but the club I work in is struggling and I said I would help the owner with some of the bills.'

'No problems I can probably move some of the money over to your bank account now. How much do you need?'

'In total fifty thousand but I think anything would help to convince the creditors to give us more time.'

'Well the most I can transfer until probate is settled is

twenty thousand. Will that help?'

'Oh yes. Thank you.'

As Jenny was leaving she was pushed out of the way by the same swarthy young man who had been at the club.

This time she got a much better look at him. He was about five feet ten inches tall and looked more muscular once she looked at him up close. He had eyes which were black and feral. After he entered Mr McGuffin's room Jenny turned to the receptionist.

'Who was that rude man?'

'Oh that's Mr Smythe, he's always like that.'

'Smythe, Smythe. No relation of Veronica Smythe'

'Her son. After Veronica and Mr Swansen divorced she married Peter Smythe and they had Jet. He was spoiled as a child and when his father died I think his mother over compensated somewhat,' the receptionist blushed. 'I am so sorry I shouldn't be talking to you like this.'

'Don't worry.' Jenny smiled. 'It's just between us. Hopefully I'll see you again soon and here is my email address. If you could get Mr McGuffin to send me the files he said I needed to read, that would be brilliant.'

Chapter six – I don't like to be besides the seaside

Jenny didn't know what to do next. She needed some time to get her head around everything that had happened. Charlie had left her with a lot of responsibility and she needed to make sure she did the right thing. Two weeks ago all she had needed to worry about was making sure Mike kept the heating high enough in the club: now she had the future of Pharmcorp and The Blue Lagoon Gentlemen's club both resting on her shoulders.

She needed some time with no interruptions to think everything through so she set off for the coast for a few days where she could walk and try to get her head together. She was also hoping that Mr McGuffin would email the papers over to her so she could try and read them in peace.

This late in the year most of the campsites and holiday parks on the east coast were closed but Jenny had an old friend, from back when she was in care, with a caravan outside Skegness and she had said Jenny could borrow it whenever she liked. Jenny loved the coast at this time of the year. Everything seemed so barren and windswept, so isolated, so different from the crowds and the hustle and bustle at the height of the season.

She spent the first day wandering along the coast from
Skegness to Chapel which was about five miles. The
wind whipped around her and even though she was
wrapped up under many layers the cold bit through.
After a while Jenny reached Ingomells, which was
about half way, and was so cold she decided to find
somewhere for a warm drink. As she walked down the
main street she looked in the windows of all the cafes
and stores. All closed up for the winter, chairs on top of
tables, free papers and junk mail piling up at the bottom
of the glass doors. When her and her friend had visited
in the summer they had spent a rainy afternoon in the
bowling alley. Surely that had to be open even at this
time of the year. She got to the bowling alley and
headed upstairs to the little café. A nice cup of hot
chocolate should take some of the chill out of her bones.
As she sat there gradually warming up she checked her
emails to find one from Mr McGuffin.

Dear Miss Cartwright,
I have spoken to Mr St Johns, Mrs Smythe and Miss
Swansen and they are happy for you to receive the
shares as stated in Mr Swansen's will. These shares will
be transferred to you along with the outstanding monies
bequeathed and should be with your bank on Monday.

I have attached to this email the details of the takeover discussed with Bensons and if you need any help to understand the finer points of the deal may I suggest you talk to Mr Parker. He was an adviser that Mr Swansen sometimes used but is not well known to other parties. I have attached his details to the bottom of this email.

Thank you for your patience in this matter and if there is anything else that you require please do not hesitate to contact me. I was Charlie's lawyer and his friend for the last forty years, so if you need a sounding board please feel free to get in touch.

Yours

Mr McGuffin

Jenny could see the files were too big to open on her phone so would wait until she was back at the caravan and read everything there on her laptop. She finished her hot chocolate and stood to leave. As she did she noticed a small man getting up at the same time. He looked as if he was about to come over and talk to her. He was the sort of person who would normally have got lost in the crowd but when there was only the two of them in the place he was difficult to miss. He shook his head and rushed out of the bowling alley. How weird thought Jenny. Maybe he was just a lonely man who

53

wanted to chat and got scared. She put back on her many layers and made her way outside to walk back to the caravan.

Walking along the front she could see blue flashing lights from one of the campsites up ahead. The small man she had seen in the bowling alley came rushing towards her.

'Quick,' he called. 'The police, they're at your caravan.'

Jenny rushed after him not really thinking about who he was or how he knew where she was staying. As she approached the site she saw they were indeed at her caravan.

'Officer, what's happening here?' She called.

A serious looking PC turned and barred her way. 'Can I help you madam?'

'Yes, I am staying here. What is going on?'

'Looks like someone's broken in and caused a lot of damage. Can you have a look and see if anything's been taken?'

Jenny rushed up the steps and stopped dead in the doorway. The whole caravan had been trashed. Chair covers ripped, slashed and stuffing pulled out. As she entered she very quickly saw the rest of the caravan was in a similar state. Bed stripped and mattresses upended.

As she turned to head back outside she saw the lounge mirror, sprayed across it in large red letters "Tart, don't mess."

Jenny felt like she was going to faint but there was nowhere to sit. The PC had followed her up the steps and steadied her while grabbing a fold away chair and settling her down.

'I'm sorry Miss this must be quite a shock.'

'It sure is. Why would anyone do this?'

'It will just be youths. Having what they call fun. Can you see if anything is missing?'

'Well I don't know about my friends things. I've only borrowed the caravan for the weekend but I can see my laptop's gone.'

'Definitely youths then. They can easily sell that for drug money.'

'I'm not so sure officer. It's been a strange week.'

'Well I don't think there's much we can do. If you can wait the fingerprint boys will be here soon. I'll give you a crime number your friend can use for the insurance claim.'

'Thanks officer.'

Jenny then remembered the strange little man and looked out of the window to see him standing on the promenade. He saw her looking, tipped his hat and walked away.

Jenny returned to Nottingham that night and went straight to the club to tell the girls all about it.
'I told you there was something funny about Charlie's death and now this. It all seems a bit too coincidental not to be linked, if you ask me.' Carly said.

'It's Mindy who watches all the murder mysteries. I thought I could rely on you to be sensible.' Jenny laughed nervously.

'This is not funny Jenny; I'm worried your life might be in danger.'
'Now you are being silly. Have you been drinking the real stuff instead of Mike's watered down champagne?'
'I'm just worried about you. I've got no lectures tomorrow so why don't I come over and stay and we can have a look at the stuff Mr McGuffin sent you together.'
'Oh shit. I had forgotten all about that. My laptop has gone so I don't know how we're going to get to see it all.'
'Don't worry I've got mine in the back. I was going to study on my break, but that was before you told me all about this. I've got another two hours to go, so why don't you start looking at the stuff and once my shift's

over we can grab a pizza and some wine, go back to yours and find out what you're letting yourself in for.'

'Okay and Carly. Thanks.' Jenny smiled at her friend, glad that she had someone like Carly who she could turn to, even if she was being a bit melodramatic.

Jenny and Carly had spent most of the night reviewing the contracts and searching the internet to try to understand the points of the buyout. As far as they could tell Pharmcorp was a relatively small company with about five hundred employees and they developed new drugs and conducted clinical trials. Pharmcorp look like they were on the verge of developing something new but they did not have the resources to develop it further and needed some investment. The only way to get this investment was to merge with someone else. Bensons were the company that the merger would be with, if it went ahead, but there had been interest from Daniels, a slightly larger pharmaceutical company based on the outskirts of Nottingham. Jenny could see that the merger would be a good injection of cash but she was not sure why Terry St John was the only member of the board who wanted it.

'Morning Carly,' Jenny called as she emerged from her room, expecting to see her fast asleep on the sofa, but she was nowhere to be seen. As Jenny was looking for her phone to call Carly, the front door bell rang. Jenny rushed to answer it.

'Silly arse where have...' It wasn't Carly, It was Terry St John.

'Is that any way to greet a visitor.' he smiled

'Sorry, it was a late night and I was expecting you to be someone else.'

'I tried to call but I think your phone must be off. Can I come in?' Jenny noticed how uncomfortable he looked standing in the corridor of the flats. He kept looking over his shoulder as if he expected someone to jump out on him.

'Of course. Coffee?'

'Yes that would be marvellous.'

Jenny wandered into the lounge a few minutes later to find Terry tidying away Carly's bedding so he could sit down.

'Sorry about that, I had a friend to stay last night and I'm not quite sure where she's got to this morning.'

'Don't worry about it. It's all tidy now.' He smiled as he put the pillow on top of the neat pile he had made on the arm chair. This meant they both had to sit on the sofa and Jenny wasn't sure how comfortable she was with that. At the funeral Terry St John had been courteous and kind, but that was before things started to get weird. Jenny was obviously getting Carly's paranoia, maybe it was a good job Carly had vanished.

'I believe Mr McGuffin sent you through all the paperwork on the buyout.' He smiled again, a fatherly, trust me kind of a smile, but Jenny still wasn't comfortable.

'Yes that's right. Unfortunately the caravan I was staying in over the weekend was trashed last night and my laptop was stolen.'

'Oh my, you poor girl. Are you okay?' He seemed genuinely concerned and Jenny started to relax.

'Yes luckily I was out at the time but the caravan belonged to a friend and it's been trashed.' She didn't tell him about the little man. She didn't know why but so far she hadn't told anyone about the little man.

'Well as long as you're alright and I see you have managed to replace it.' He pointed to Carly's laptop open on the coffee table. 'The joys of coming into some money hey?'

'That belongs to my friend.' Jenny was quite indignant that he could suggest she was wasting money just because she was suddenly rich. 'I shall wait for the insurance to come through before I replace mine.'

'Very frugal.' He nodded. 'Have you had time to look at the contract?'

'Yes. I have a few questions but I want to do my own research if that is okay? After all you do have a vested interest in my decision.'

'I completely understand. It's very commendable that you're trying to do your own research, but let me just say that this buyout is one of the best things that could happen to Pharmcorp. The development of the latest drug will be lost without it, and that could have massive impact on the population. This drug could be the next step in curing the common cold. Imagine how much easier life would be if that happened. Hopefully it can be developed further to cure flu. Now that would be a breakthrough.'

'You keep calling it a buyout but I thought it was

supposed to be a merger.'

'Well that was the original plan, but with Charlie

gone… well a buyout seems a better plan. I would have

thought Vicki would have preferred a merger so she

could stay with the project but she's opposed to the

sale.'

'And why did Charlie want a merger?'

'To give Vicki a future and protect the workforce. He

was always going to retire when the deal was done.'

'What would happen to the staff at Pharmcorp?'
'Most of them would keep their jobs, I suppose. They have the expertise. I'm not really sure, Bensons will need to sort all that out.'

'Well thanks for popping round, Mr St John. I'll let you know if I need anything else.'

'Okay but remember, this is what Charlie wanted, he started this deal after all, and please call me Terry.'

The door opened and in walked Carly carrying two MacDonald's breakfasts and two large cappuccinos.

'That's where you got to,' Jenny smiled, 'I was starting to worry.'

Jenny was glad Carly had come back. There was something she didn't trust about Terry St John but Charlie trusted him so maybe he was okay.

'Well I'll be off then and let you enjoy your breakfast.'

'Thanks, and I'll call if I need anything.' Jenny smiled as he left. She was glad he was gone.

Carly stayed until lunchtime when she got a call from the hospital saying there was going to be an important operation that she could view, if she wanted too. She rushed off telling Jenny to call if there were any problems. Jenny decided to try and understand the buyout paperwork again and write down any questions she needed to ask Mr Parker. She certainly wasn't going to ask Terry St John, he was the sort of person who could convince you black was white if it suited his needs. Jenny had finished her list of questions and was thinking about going out to get something to eat when the phone rang.

'Jenny here.'

'Oh hi Jenny. Its Vicki Swansen, I was wondering if you had time to meet up this afternoon for a chat?' Vicki Swansen sounded as self assured as she looked.

'Well I was about to go out for something to eat, but you could meet me if you like.'

'Oh brilliant, whereabouts?'

'Do you know Holly's Café on Upper Parliament Street?'

'No but I'm sure I can find it. I should be there in about thirty minutes if that's okay.'

'Fine see you there.'

Jenny grabbed her bag, phone and the papers from Mr McGuffin she had printed and walked down to Holly's Café, a throwback to different age in Nottingham. Most of the shops around it had gone, either knocked down or just replaced by newer better looking establishments. The cafe had been run by the same man as long as Jenny could remember, and that was thirty years ago when her mum used to take her in for a milkshake to shut her up, assuming her mum had made some money the night before and not spent it on drugs.

She walked in and marvelled at the improvements that had been made over the years. It had been expanded and modernised, it no longer had the ripped faux leather booths and nicotine stained ceiling. Instead it now had wooden floors and was light and airy. But it did still have tomato ketchup in squeazy bottles the shape of tomatoes and the smell of chip fat permeated everything in the place.

While she was placing her order, Jenny chatted with the waitress. They didn't know each other but that was just the way it was in here. Everyone had time to engage with everyone else; people made eye contact and smiled. Not the sort of place you could sit undisturbed and read documents without someone coming to check you were alright. Jenny ordered a raspberry milkshake and egg and chips and went and sat by the window. The egg and chips arrived at the same time as Vicki and the look on her face nearly made Jenny wish she hadn't suggested meeting here. Only nearly mind you.

'Hi Vicki,' called Jenny waving.

'Oh erm hi Jenny, how are you?' Jenny felt good that the self assured business woman was not as confident as she looked, especially when out of her comfort zone.

'Good thanks. I hope you don't mind but I ordered already, I didn't know if you wanted to eat.'

64

Vicki looked at Jenny's plate and gagged. 'Think just a Macchiato for me thanks.'

'Well if you pop down to the counter at the back she will make one for you. I don't think they do Macchiatos;

just ask for a milky coffee. They're great.'

Vicki wandered down to the back of the cafe and ordered her coffee. Wandering back she had to walk extra slow as the mug was full to overflowing and very hot.

'So Vicki what can I do for you?' Jenny asked as she took another mouthful of egg and chips.

'I just wanted to check you were okay really, I know you were very close to my father.' Vicki smiled and took a sip of her coffee, carefully placing the mug on the table, she sucked in cooling air.

'Thank you for asking. Yes I am okay thank you. I had known him for a long time and it came as a great shock. But what about you?'

'Well I think I knew he was wearing himself out. The doctor had said he was okay when he had his physical a few weeks back but he had put so much work into this buyout that I think he must have burnt himself out.'

'I guess that's why you don't want the buyout to go through then, you feel it killed your father.'

'Well I think it did but that's not the reason. I think we could manage by ourselves. There is no guarantee that the staff will keep their jobs and that was always the most important thing for Dad. We can generate the extra cash by having a shares issue. It would dilute the power of the current share holders but surely it's better to still

have the majority of control over the company than no control over what Bensons do with our research.' Vicki was very animated in her explanation and Jenny could see how passionate she was about the company. 'I know

I would be able to push everything through. I just need to get the board to appoint me Chief Executive Office and we could really be onto a winner.'
'So who is in charge at the moment?' Jenny was confused as she thought that Terry St John was looking after the day to day running of the company.

'Terry for the time being but only because he's the Chief Finance Officer, the board has to appoint a new CEO before the buyout can go ahead.'
'Do you know why Daniels pulled out of the talks?'
'No I'm not sure. Dad and Terry went to see them and everything was going great until about three days before the sealed bids were due. They just rang up and said

they didn't want to enter a bid.'

'It would be interesting to find out what turned them against the deal.'

'Sure would. I tell you what why don't I pop into the office and see if there is anything in Dad's papers. I can check out his office at home as well to see if that gives us any clues.'

'Great. Terry St John told me that Pharmcorp didn't have the ability to develop the drug and that the technology could be lost if Bensons don't buy us out.'

'Buy US out? So you're part of the team then.'

'Of course. Charlie gave me these shares to make sure we do what's right, but I'm not in this alone. We need to work together to get the best for everyone,' Jenny said.

'On that note did you talk to Terry St John about what would happen to the staff?'

'Yes I did and he didn't seem overly concerned.'

'That sounds like Terry. He's right if this drug isn't developed that would be a massive loss to science and possibly civilisation but did he mention that he's in line for over a billion pounds if this deal goes through.'

'What,' Jenny stared at Vicki with her mouth wide open and the last piece of egg clinging precariously to her fork.

'Exactly Terry's far more concerned with closing the deal and making the money than saving western civilisation from the possible terrorist threat of the flu.'

67

'Sorry. Terrorist threat. What are you talking about?'
Jenny was getting more and more confused.

'Well it is believed in some quarters that the next big terrorist threat will be a virus. In 1918 Spanish flu killed 50 million people, 3% of the population at the time. If that virus was released in a major city, the effect would be devastating. We believe that this drug could be used to fight something as dangerous as Spanish flu but it needs more development.'

'In that case you have to let Bensons take it they have far more resources than you and they could develop it much faster.'

'I see why you would think that but it's not the case. They would develop the drug enough to cure the common cold because the income from that would be huge. Why bother spending the extra money to cure flu if there is no money in it?'

'This all sounds like stuff of fantasy and spy books.'

'It is, but that is the way it goes. You need to think very hard before you make any sort of decision.'

'I will.'

'Thanks for listening to my side of the argument.' Vicki smiled. 'I think I can see why my father trusted you. Just make sure you have all the facts before you make your final decision.'

Vicki rose and shook Jenny's hand, 'and thanks for the coffee, you were right it was great, if not a little hot.'

Jenny was very confused but she wanted more information before she was prepared to make any decision and she thought she knew exactly the right person to ask. All she had to do now was work out how to get an appointment with Richard Pickle, the Chief Executive Officer of Daniels.

Chapter eight – Cecil & Richard

Cecil Moreau could not believe his luck when the will was read. He had been left CVV publishing and all he had to do was not change the name. He had looked around the room nervously, sure that someone would object that he, a lowly secretary, should be left a whole publishing house but they had not even batted an eyelid. They were more concerned that the stripper had got seven percent of the shares in Pharmcorp. 'I mean seven percent, what damage could she possibly do with that?'Cecil thought.

Cecil had loved literature at school and studied English Literature at Nottingham Trent University. Unfortunately he enjoyed university life a little too much, and had been kicked off the course at the end of the second year. This hadn't stopped him putting a first on his CV. No-one ever checked CV's in detail these days and as long as you were good at your job why would they? He first met Charlie at a book festival in Hay on Wye and after chatting for a few hours, Charlie offered him a lift back to Nottingham. The limo was a definite improvement upon eight hours of slow trains and dirty waiting rooms. They had spent the whole journey discussing their love of literature and how they both had at some point in their lives wished to be an author, but realised they didn't have the talent. Charlie also told Cecil about the small publishing house he had bought in the early eighties. He had renamed it CVV which stood for Charlie, Veronica and Vicki. He set it up with dreams of competing with Bloomsbury and the like, but he had not realised how much work was involved and had turned it into a house that helped young or new authors publish their first novels instead. It had never made any money and Charlie was such a soft touch when it came to authors, more often than not it made a loss. Charlie didn't mind because he felt he was adding something to the literary world and the loss could be offset against Pharmcorp's massive profits for tax, so everyone was happy.

Six months after this first meeting Cecil was desperate for work. He was surviving on a little temping work here and there but the money was not supporting his party life style. Then out of the blue he got a call from Charlie. Charlie's secretary was going off on maternity leave and he needed someone to look after him. Would Cecil like to cover the job until she came back? Cecil jumped at the chance, the work was mainly looking after Charlie's appointments and making sure no one got to Charlie, if he didn't want them to. After nine months the previous secretary decided that she liked being a stay at home mum and the job was made permanent. Cecil made himself invaluable to Charlie and stayed. Soon Cecil had such a good system going with Charlie, he asked if in his spare time he could look into the publishing house. Charlie loved the idea and Cecil was given one day a week, where Charlie bought in a temp to take on some of Cecil's more menial tasks, and let

him focus on the publishing house.

Cecil loved it and was soon interviewing writers and agents, to make sure the publishing house got some people who could write, and not just people who thought they could. By the end of the first year under Cecil's influence, the publishing house had broken even. Two years later it made a small profit. Whilst Charlie was pleased about the money, he was more pleased that the publishing house was starting to take off. Just before he died Charlie had been looking for a new secretary so Cecil could work on it full time. Their latest coup was they had one of the books on the Booker long list. If it made the shortlist it would mean massive publicity for the publishing house as well as the author. CVV could really start going somewhere.

Cecil had seen the stripper at the funeral and had always wondered what made a girl do that kind of job. She was good looking in a plain way and apart from the long hair and fantastic legs, not what he had expected in a stripper. He always thought you would be able to spot a stripper a mile off but she looked normal, plain almost. He also needed a celebration for one of his minor celebrity authors, who had competed in Big Brother seven years ago, and had written a book about his fall from grace and return to normal life. None of the big publishing houses would touch him, but Cecil liked him and decided to run with it. So in an effort to kill two birds with one stone Cecil arranged for a night out at the Blue Lagoon Gentleman's Club.

Jenny never worked Saturday nights but since Carly had got so paranoid and as all three of her best friends were working Jenny decided to hang out at the club. It was unusually busy and one of the other girls had rung in sick, so Mike asked Jenny if she wouldn't mind working a shift. One of the tables was particularly raucous and populated by a group of men who were a little older, than the usual stag do's the Blue Lagoon attracted on a Saturday night. She did a double take as she took the order, convinced that she recognised the guy at the head of the table. He was towering above the other guys, he kept standing up and waving his money around while all the other guys stayed seated. His slicked back hair and red braces reminded her of something from Wall

Street, but the Charlie Sheen character not the Michael Douglas one. As she brought the drinks back to the table she realised who he was.

'Hi, its Cecil isn't it?' She shouted trying to make herself heard above the pounding sounds of Tina Turner

'Yes that's right.. umm … Jenny right?' He smiled at the rest of the group.

'Wow good memory.'

The music died and Jenny was relieved she could stop shouting, even if only for a few moments

'I was actually hoping to see you. I don't know if you remember but Charlie left me his publishing house and I am trying to build it up. It was a hobby for Charlie and it's been left to stagnate and I want to try to pick it up out of the gutter.'

'Well I'm afraid I can't invest, I'm too tied up in this thing with Pharmcorp at the moment.'

'Oh no I don't need any money. Well not for the time being anyway. I was hoping to buy your story. You know how you came to be a stripper and what it's like.'

'Wow I'm not sure I would want to do that. It seems a little intrusive.'

'But assuming the book took off there could be some money in it and no-one else is doing anything like it at the moment.' He smiled. Jenny felt quite sorry for him.

74

It sounded as if he had been left something that wasn't worth anything unless he worked really hard and then maybe he could turn it around.

'I tell you what, let me talk to the girls and see if any of them are interested in selling their story. Some of their stories are a lot more interesting than mine, and they could probably do with the money more than I can.'

'Thanks. If you get any interest get them to pop into the office. I'm free all day Monday so anytime will do,' he handed Jenny his card and returned to his friends.

The following day Jenny was still trying to work out how to get an appointment with Richard Pickles. She had tried the website of Daniels and unsurprisingly his details were not made public. When she rang the office she was told that Mr Pickles was unavailable, he was fully booked for the next three weeks. She could try to make an appointment after that, but that would be too late as the board meeting was in two weeks. However whilst doing her research she did find out that he had been involved in a skiing accident some years back where Peter Smythe had been killed. Jenny wondered if that Peter Smythe could have been the same man Veronica had been married to. Vicki had been keen for her to get all the facts before she made a decision and

Veronica had been so kind to her, she decided to give Veronica a call to see if she could help.

'Veronica Smythe.' Veronica answered the phone, in a no nonsense don't try to sell me something kind of a way.

'Veronica, its Jenny Cartwright here.'

'Oh hi Jenny how are you?'

'Good, thank you. And you?'

'Yes not too bad. I have been trying to help Marissa sort out Charlie's things but the poor girl has gone to pieces. Anyway what can I do for you?'

'I was talking to Vicki last week about the buyout and she suggested I should get all the information before I make a decision.'

'Sensible girl my Vicki.'

'I would like to talk to the Daniels chief executive office to understand why they pulled out of the deal.'

'Makes sense.'

'I can't get hold of him, but I think you might know him personally, and I was wondering if you could get me an introduction.'

'Hmm, I did used to know him but we haven't spoken since the accident. You see Charlie and Terry were sorting out the buyout, I was just waiting for them to give me all the information once they were ready for the board to make a decision. Can't you ask Terry?'

'I would but I don't really want Mr St John to know how much research I am doing. Sorry if that sounds bad.'

'No I completely understand my dear. Leave it with me and I will see what I can do.'

'Thank you so much.'

Chapter nine – What makes a nice girl become a stripper?

The following day Jenny, Carly, Blossom and Mindy headed off to meet Cecil Moreau and discuss whether he would be interested their stories.

The office was much more impressive that Jenny had expected it to be. It was in a new development on Castle Boulevard and looked out over the canal and the tax offices. As the girls walked in to the reception their heels broke the silence as they clipped across the wooden floor towards a tall reception desk. The perfectly coiffured receptionist looked very efficient in her space age headset. As the ladies entered the receptionist gave them a look that said 'don't even

bother'.

'Can I help you erm, ladies?' she asked. 'One moment.' She held up a finger and turned her head and spoke into her headset. They hadn't even heard the telephone ring

but they were still left standing whilst she directed the call.

'Sorry about that ladies, now what can I do for you?'

'We have an appointment with Mr Moreau,' Jenny smiled as sweetly as she could.

'Are you sure? I have nothing in the diary.'

'Well he made the appointment himself on Saturday. Maybe you could check.'

'The receptionist turned her back on them and started to make a phone call, as Cecil Moreau appeared on the gantry above their heads.

'Jenny, ladies, so glad you could make it,' he called down. 'Suzy gets the ladies some drinks and make them comfortable in my office. Jenny I'll be there in two minutes, just got to sort this out first,' he waved a mobile phone in the air.

Suzy became the model of professionalism, now she knew Cecil had invited them to the office. Up above Jenny could hear Cecil talking to someone and from the tone of the conversation she guessed it was an author.

'Listen Jenkins, the idea's a good one but you just don't have the skill to pull it off. If we published everyone who walks through that door we'd never make any money. Yes of course I'll send the manuscript and the map back. It'll be in the next post, don't you worry.'

The ladies were led into Cecil's office. They settled down on a soft leather three piece suite and as Suzy handed them their drinks they hesitated, unsure whether the glass coffee table was there as decoration or to be used.

'Hi there ladies,' Cecil powered into the room.

'Hi Cecil,' smiled Jenny. 'Can I introduce you to Blossom, Mindy and Carly? The girls work with me and Blossom and Mindy thought it might be worthwhile having a chat with you about your idea. Although I must say this is not what I expected from a struggling publishing house.'

'No, I am very lucky that this was Charlie's baby. He bought and furnished the offices himself when he first had the idea of setting up a publishing house. He wanted us to look the part from day one.'

'Well that certainly explains the swish offices.'

'Excellent news about you guys talking to me about your stories. You not interested though Jenny or you Carly?'

'My story is hardly worth it Mr Moreau,' said Carly. 'I am just a normal person studying and trying to get through medical school without building up a ridiculous amount of debt. Hardly block buster material.'

'Call me Cecil. I do see what you mean. Maybe we could do a smaller piece on the ways people try to survive university in these modern times and I could include you in that.'

'Not sure my parents would enjoy that. I'm here as moral support for Blossom and Mindy.' Carly smiled and took a sip of the cappuccino.

'And you Jenny? It's a story worth telling, from stripper

to wealthy business women, and soon to be owner of

her own club if the rumours are to be believed.' The

other girls all turned to stare at Jenny. How did Cecil

know she was planning to buy the club when she hadn't

even told the girls yet?

 'How did you get into stripping?'

'That's not really important and I'm not sure what you've

heard but nothing's settled about me and the club yet.'

Jenny wasn't sure whether she liked Cecil or not but she

did know she didn't trust him. 'You need to talk to

Mindy and Blossom they really do have stories worth

telling.'

'Of course. Blossom why don't you start?'

'Well it's a bit hazy but I can give you the general idea.'

Blossom was looking every bit the stripper in a black

cat suit, which clung to every curve and contour of her

body, four inch heels and bright blue eye shadow. She

had also opted for her favourite electric blue wig which

was in the shape of a bob and framed her chiselled

cheek bones.

'It started when I was about fourteen, my boyfriend of

the time convinced me to go to a concert with him in

London. We met up with some really cool people and

smoked some dope ,and before I knew it we had been

away for a week. My dad was one of those West Indian fathers who are not to be messed with when he was angry, and I was petrified about going home, my mum died when I was very small so I would have had to face his wrath alone.' Blossom looked around the girls and gave them a nervous smile.

'My boyfriend promised he would look after me so we stayed in this squat in London for about six weeks. Then the little money we had ran out. He had friends in Nottingham, and it was cheaper to live up here, so we moved and found another squat. By this time we were smoking a lot of dope. We progressed to the hard stuff, I can't really remember when but within weeks we had no money and no way of getting any.'

Jenny patted Blossom's hand as she stopped for a few seconds. 'Are you sure you want to go on?'

Blossom nodded and continued talking, focusing on her feet as she did. 'Ste, my boyfriend, did a couple of burglaries to get us some cash but then things got a bit heavy. He arrived home one night with Nigel. I don't think Nigel was the guy's real name, we had a bit of a party back at the flat. Once I had had too much to drink Nigel got out the scank. He said he only shared it with girls who were good to him, and if I was good to him he would let me have some. I couldn't think. I was so desperate for the drugs that I would agree to anything. He said he'd let me have some if I gave him a blow job. Obviously I was worried Ste was there and I loved him, but I was desperate. Ste said it would be okay as it wasn't like I was cheating on him 'cause he was there. We'd had plenty to drink so I did what Nigel asked and then we got the drugs.

'The next morning I couldn't believe what I'd done. I decided I had sunk too low and I had to get out. I knew Dad would go ape but if I explained I was sure he would forgive me. I waited until Ste woke up and I told him what I was going to do. "I don't think you will, you're going stay here and help me." Ste said. When I said I couldn't anymore Ste showed me a video from the night before. He had filmed the whole thing on his mobile. "Do you want your precious daddy to see this?" he yelled. I couldn't let my dad see the video. He would never forgive me. I knew I was trapped. From then on things got worse. Ste would bring different men into my room each night and I would do whatever they asked. I never saw any money and Ste would bring me drugs and occasionally some food.' Blossom raised her head and looked at her audience, each in turn. Only Cecil didn't hold her gaze.

'I didn't know how I was going to get out and then one day Mike from the club turned up. I didn't know who he was, I thought he was just another punter. He told me to get dressed and started to carry me out of the flat just as Ste turned up. When Ste tried to stop him, Mike told him he had won me fair and square and there was nothing Ste could do about it. I didn't know what to think as it was starting to sound like something out of the slave trade. Ste argued some more and eventually Mike put me down on the couch and hit Ste so hard I don't know if he ever woke up. Mike picked me up and took me out to his car. From there he drove me straight to a rehab centre. Throughout my treatment he visited be most weeks and once I was clean he offered me a job. I never finished school and I can't do anything else so I thought I would give it a try. I don't think I'll ever me able to face my dad, but at least now I am away from Ste and everything he put me through. Whilst Mike's about I know I'll be okay.'

As she stopped the other girls gathered round her and enveloped her in a massive hug.

'You've got us too,' Mindy said holding her close.

'Wow what an amazing story.' Cecil smiled. 'I would

love to see if we could do something with that. If we do

it right there might even be a potential movie deal, who

would you like to play you?'

'Really you think we could do that?' Blossom dried her

eyes and stared at him.

'A story like yours is so heartbreaking and because it's

true people will lap it up.' Cecil got up and poured

Blossom a glass of water.

'Perhaps we should just think about a book first.' Carly

said. 'There's no need to get over excited at this stage is

there?'

Blossom frowned and stuck her bottom lip out.

'Now Mindy what about you?' Cecil smiled and gently

touched her hand.

Mindy swallowed hard and began, 'I was born just two

days after Sunil's tenth birthday. My parents and his

parents had been friends ever since they had first come

to this country as children. I had a fairly normal

childhood, but it was always expected that I would

marry and stay at home to look after the children. None

of the other women in our circle of friends or family had ever done anything other than be home makers. I was promised to Sunil when I was twelve and he had already been to college and was looking for a career. Sunil was a businessman who bought and sold things, but no-one in the family knew exactly what he did. He always returned from business trips with gifts for his mother, my mother and me. Once I finished school at sixteen, I was determined to go on and study, I'd always

wanted to do something more than just look after a family. It was frowned upon and more and more pressure was put on me to marry Sunil. I decide from what little I knew of Sunil, there was more chance of me going to college if I was his wife, than if I stayed at home. He was very modern and I thought we could grow together like any other English couple. Sunil and I were married the day of my sixteenth birthday and for the first few months we lived with his parents.

'Most of the time Sunil was away on his business trips

and then one day after he'd been away for three weeks he returned and had a massive row with his dad. They

spoke Hindi to each other. I didn't fully understand but

from the few words I knew, and things his mum had said, I worked out that someone had been chasing Sunil for money and had spoken to his dad about it. His dad had paid them. Sunil went mad. The next day we had moved out into our own place. For about six month's it was great. I cooked all Sunil's favourite food and looked after the house. Sunil always gave me plenty of money to get nice things, he liked me to look my best. I spoke to Sunil about starting college and he had said that I could look at the prospectus of the local college and then we could talk about what would be best.

'Then one afternoon a man about Sunil's age turned up and said Sunil had told him to come to the house to meet him. I knew Sunil was due back anytime so I let the man in and was just serving him some tea when Sunil arrived. I was quickly pushed into the kitchen and I have no idea what happened. After the man had left Sunil came into the kitchen and hit me for the first time. He told me never to ever let anyone in and not to show them the honour of serving them tea in his house. I ignored the slap, he was very angry and I had obviously done something very wrong. Whenever I tried to talk about going to college after that, he said I was too stupid to go, and he didn't want the world to know how stupid his wife was.

'Sunil would stay out late, sometimes all night and if he did come home it would be late but he would always expect his diner to be ready. I never knew when he would get home so I often got a slap for the dinner either not being ready or being dried out because it had been ready hours before. After we had been married a year I discovered I was pregnant. I was not sure how I felt about it, I was obviously happy to be pregnant but the beatings were getting more and more regular. Sunil was so happy when I told him that suddenly it was like he was a different person. An heir was all he could think of. Things improved, he treated me like a princess and nothing was too much trouble. He even talked about getting a maid to help out so I could rest and look after the baby.

'When I was 28 weeks pregnant I was chatting to the milkman one morning as Sunil arrived home. "You might want to leave my wife alone you white bastard." he had screamed at the milkman, before pushing him over and slamming the door. He was drunk and dragged me upstairs when he "taught me a lesson" for making him look foolish in front of the neighbours. After I had given up trying to explain and was starting to feel lightheaded from the beating, he decided it was time for sex. I couldn't believe he had just finished beating me and now he wanted to make love to me. Only he didn't. He pinned me down, and held me there. I tried to struggle but I was already exhausted from the beating. He ripped my sari and pinned me down. He was pushing down on me so hard that he struggled to get his trousers undone, but he was determined not to let me go. It was over in seconds and he rolled off me and went to sleep. I didn't know what to do. I lay on the bed next to him, crying but trying not to make too much noise. I didn't want to wake him.' Mindy stopped and gulped in mouthfuls of air.

Blossom grabbed her hand and held it tight. 'You are so brave. Why have you never told me this before? I'm sure Mike will be able to sort the little shit out.'

'That's not the worst of it,' Mindy said.

'Are you sure you want to carry on?' Jenny asked.

'I think it's time the girls knew the rest don't you Jenny?' Mindy said

'As long as you feel up to it. You can stop whenever you want.'

'Sure.' Mindy took a sip of her cappuccino and continued her story. 'After the rape I knew I needed some help so I took my mobile and locked myself in the bathroom while I rang my mum. I was in such a state on the phone that she rushed over to see what the problem was. By the time she got there I had not got dressed and she could see what Sunil had done to me.

"Don't be silly," she said. "You must have done

something wrong. Sunil is the master of this house and you need to learn to live by his rules and look after him. You always were too headstrong. You were lucky to get Sunil. There were other girls interested you know. Your father and I had to do a lot of work to make sure you

were top of the list."

"But he has just beaten and raped me. I can't stay here." I cried.

"So you would leave and bring dishonour to your

mother and father? After all we have done. You need to

show your husband some respect." She said.

'I couldn't believe my own mother wouldn't help me, I

had no idea how to get out of the situation. I had nowhere to turn. I had to stop the beatings and the only way was to do all the things Sunil thought a good wife should do. I cooked Sunil some lunch and showered and tidied myself up, determined to do whatever I needed to do just to stop the beatings. Sunil was pleased to see I was subservient when he awoke.

'That night I awoke in agony with terrible stomach cramps and when I turned the lights on I was covered in blood. Not knowing what to do or who to turn to - Sunil had gone out again - I rang an ambulance. At the hospital I was rushed into surgery and they had to operate, I had lost more blood that they first thought. I lost the baby and they had to perform a hysterectomy to save my life.' Mindy stroked her stomach.

'The next day was the first time I met Jenny as she was visiting someone in the same ward. Jenny was helping battered women. She was talking to one of the women who had returned to her husband from the hostel, after he had sweet talked her and now she was back in hospital. I didn't really pay her much attention at the time but I remember thinking if there was a way out why would you go back, and wishing I had a way out.

'I had not had time to leave a note for Sunil about where I was so rang him almost every hour the first day I was in hospital. It took until that evening for me to finally get through to him. He said he would come to the hospital as soon as he could. It was another three days before he turned up. At first he was very kind and said

91

we could try again for another baby. He didn't mention that it was his beating that had caused me to lose the baby. Then when I told him about the hysterectomy I thought he was going to lose it. He held his temper, just.

Luckily for me I was on a public ward. "You are of no

use to me now are you?" he whispered in my ear and he

left, only turning back, at the entrance to the ward, with a look of sheer hatred in his eyes. Two days later a bin bag full of my clothes appeared. I knew there was no point me going home, so I rang my mum. I couldn't believe it when Sunil answered the phone.

"I've explained everything to your parents and they

think I did the right thing throwing you out. Don't try to

contact them again." He said before slamming down the phone.

'I couldn't believe it. My parents would rather console a wife beater than their own daughter. The next day Jenny turned up to see someone else and I plucked up the courage to ask her if she knew anyone who could help. She got me a place at the hostel; I was ready to leave hospital but wouldn't be able to look for work for at least six weeks. Over those six weeks I saw Jenny quite a few times and we got chatting. It was obvious that I had no skills and was going to struggle to get work. I went to meet her from work one day and after

everything I'd been through, working in the club didn't

look too bad. One of the other girls had left to get married so there was an opening. I started behind the bar and then as a waitress in a corset and suspenders and then moved on to stripping about three months ago. I know my parents will never speak to me again, but I do hope one day to see my brother again and explain what really happened.'

Cecil was silent after she finished.

'Any chance of another Cappuccino?' Carly asked a few

minutes later finally breaking the oppressive silence. After the girls had enjoyed their drinks they left promising to keep in touch with Cecil and he promised to find a ghost writer who could turn their stories into blockbusters. Blossom and Mindy were excitedly talking about who would play them in the movie and how they could be as rich as J K Rowling when Jenny's phone rang.

'Jenny speaking,' after a short pause she smiled, 'Thanks Veronica.'

'What's that?' Carly asks.

'Veronica's got me an appointment with Richard Pickles tomorrow. Time to find out what's so weird about this deal.'

Chapter ten – Mr Pickles I presume

Blossom and Mindy were excitedly chatting about their potential book deals when they arrived at the club that night. As they walked up to the rear entrance Mindy was sent flying by a tall dark man rushing out from the back doors.

'Oi watch it arsehole,' shouted Blossom as she ran to pick up her friend. 'Are you okay sweetie?'

'Yes I think so. I could do without a bruised arse before the show.'

'Don't worry I'll powder it for you.' Blossom grinned

'It's any excuse with you isn't it?'

'Can you blame me? You're a mighty fine looking woman,' Blossom said in her best American drawl.

'Help me up and let's get to work.'

The girls rushed inside still giggling and bumped into Mike as he opened the back door.

'You okay girls?' He asked.

'Yes thanks we are going to be authors according to Jenny's friend.'

'Really I'd like to see that.' Mike looked around and hustled the girls into the dressing room.

Jenny was sat at the front of the club talking to Mike, as Blossom and Mindy came on to do their show. They were still grinning from ear to ear and as they both started to swing on their poles, they seemed to be enjoying the show more than usual.

'The money is all sorted now, so we can talk to the solicitors tomorrow about funding the club, and me becoming a partner if you like Mike.' Jenny shouted above the sounds of Tina Turner's Private Dancer blasting out from the speakers on the stage.

'I've been thinking about that and I'd rather you just bought me out.' Mike said.

'But Mike I need you to help me. I can't do this on my own.' Jenny's face dropped. She had thought she was just helping Mike out of a hole. She hadn't planned on running the whole thing by herself.

'Don't worry, I'll help you out until you get on your feet and you can still employ me as a bouncer if you like. I just don't enjoy it anymore. The last few weeks have been really tough and I don't need the hassle at my age.'

'Come on Mike, we all love you and we couldn't get by without you.' Jenny noticed the smoke from the stage show had suddenly got much thicker than usually. It was getting hard to see the girls, and that wasn't really the point of the show. Mike must have noticed about the same time and vanished into the back. Suddenly there were sparks and the smell of burning permeating the air.

One of the sparks caught the curtains and flames were licking the side of the stage within seconds. Jenny smashed the fire alarm on the wall by the bar and started shouting for everyone to clear out. The majority of the punters headed towards the front exit and within seconds the door was blocked. The girls had all headed towards the staff entrance at the back.

'Follow me guys,' Mindy called to a group of lads that were near the stage. They were standing by their table looking around. 'Guys, guys. This way,' Mindy called again and finally they started to move towards the back door. Some of the people at the back of the crowd pushing towards the front door turned and seeing the girls heading for the back door ran in that direction. Jenny couldn't find Blossom in the smoke. She knew Mindy had headed towards the back and hoped she had made it out okay, but there had been no sign of Blossom since the stampede had started. As Jenny squinted to try and see through the smoke she could hear some sirens outside. She hoped they were heading her way. Jenny headed towards the stage. She couldn't leave without checking just in case Blossom was there. She covered her mouth with her scarf and bending over ,to get as low as possible, headed towards the stage. As she fought through the smoke she could make out a shape slumped on the floor. It was Blossom. She was unconscious. Jenny grabbed hold of her and tried to drag her towards the door. The noise of people had died down and Jenny could only hope everyone had made it out. The smoke was making it difficult to see and she needed to get Blossom outside. For a skinny black woman she was sure difficult to move. Jenny was dragging her in the direction of the back door, or at least the direction she thought the back door was in. Out of nowhere appeared a huge yellow figure, the mask covering his face making it impossible to see who or what it was. As he approached the girls Jenny could hear his breathing. She stopped and stared at him. He reached towards her, then she was falling and Blossom landed on top of her.

Jenny came too in the back of an ambulance. The paramedic checked her pulse and grabbed her hand to stop her removing the oxygen mask.

'It's okay. We're just taking you to the hospital. You've swallowed some smoke so you need checking out.'

'Blo-Blo-Blossom.' Jenny strained to get the word out.

'Is that one of your friends?' the paramedic asked. 'There were other people brought out so we can check once we get to the hospital.'

Jenny lay back, praying Blossom was okay.

The next thing Jenny remembered was waking up in a ward.

'She's awake,' Carly's voice whispered. 'Hi there sweetie, you had us worried for a minute there.'

Jenny tried to speak but found her throat was too sore and dry for the words to form.

'Throat a bit dry?' Carly had been on duty and had stayed on to check on her friends. 'Don't worry. Try and drink some of this water. Mindy's here so she will stay with you whilst I go and check on Blossom.'

As Carly walked away Mindy sat down next to Jenny. 'Oh Jenny, I am so glad you are okay. You were so brave staying in there to help Blossom.' Mindy was crying. She tried but failed to look Jenny in the eye. 'I just ran out, I didn't think of anyone but myself. I'm so sorry.'

Jenny grabbed her hand and smiled, she had been the stupid one nearly getting herself killed.

'Blossom?'

'She's in a pretty bad way. Part of the scenery must have fallen on her. She has a concussion and a massive lump on the back of her head and she's got a lot of smoke on her lungs. It's a good job you went to get her. They would never have found her without you.'

'Mike?' Jenny realised he had rushed off when the fire started and she was worried he might have been caught somewhere.

'No sign of him. There are happy they got everyone out of the building but no-one knows what happened to him. Blossom and I saw a guy running from the building as we arrived and Mike looked worried when we saw him before the show. I think something weird is going on.'

Jenny wanted to talk more to her friend but the strain on her throat was just too much. She held Mindy's hand a little longer and then lay back, too exhausted to even think about what had happened.

The next day Jenny felt much better and was discharged with some antibiotics and told to rest for the next few days. She went to visit Blossom and was glad to see she was awake.

'Hey there how you doing,' Jenny smiled

Blossom smiled back. 'Not too bad,' she croaked.

'They've told me not to talk too much, and I've got to stay in for the next few days because of the concussion.'

'Okay, Listen I think something weird is going on but I need to find Mike first. The guy you and Mindy saw leaving the club, and the fact you have a bump on the back of your head when there was no fallen scenery anywhere near you, makes me think Mike is in more trouble than he let on. Let me find him before you talk to the police.'

'Can't talk, bad throat.' Blossom winced and winked.

'Good girl. I'll come back later and let you know what I've found out.'

Jenny had no idea where Mike would be, so she headed home to think about what to do next. As the bus pulled into the town square Jenny decided to go and have a look at the devastation before walking the rest of the way home. As she walked up Angel Row she couldn't believe it. The Southern Fried Chicken place on the end of Hurts Yard looked as it always did. You would never have known there had been a fire. She turned up Hurts Yard. The club front was the same as always except the door was open and the little she could see inside looked like a blackened shell. The smell was the worst thing, burning suede and nylon hanging in the air. At least nothing other than material items had been lost. Everyone had got out safely even if a few were battered and bruised.

Jenny's phone rang, it was Veronica.

'Jenny, where are you? I went to all the trouble of getting you a meeting with Richard Pickle and you don't bother showing up. Thanks for that. Do you know how difficult it was for me to contact him?' As Veronica paused for breath Jenny jumped in.

'Veronica, I'm so sorry I forgot all about it. You see there was a fire at the club last night.'

'Oh God, I didn't know. Are you okay?'

'I was in hospital all night. They've said I'm okay but one of my best friends is still in a bad way. I had to make sure she was alright.'

'Of course you did. I am so sorry, I didn't mean to shout, it's just with everything that's happened, speaking to Richard brought up some bad memories. Do you still want to meet him?'

'Yes I do.'

'When I spoke to him earlier he said he was only in the office this morning, and then he was leaving the country for four weeks. If you hurry you might just make it in time.'

'Okay, I'll jump in a taxi straight away. Is he at the main offices out on Thane Road?'

'Yes that's right. I hope you get what you need from him.'

'I will do, and thanks for your help Veronica, I know it can't have been easy.'

Jenny ran out of Hurt's Yard and grabbed a taxi, she couldn't afford to let this opportunity go, finding Mike would have to wait.

As Jenny arrived at Daniels' head office she had to wait whilst the guard checked that she was expected. He pointed out she was over three hours late, but as she was on the list he would let her in. The taxi was flagged through and told to go to the nearest building. Jenny hopped out of the taxi and headed into a large building made almost completely of glass. It wasn't until she got inside, that she realised it was one way glass as she could see the wonderful landscaped garden surrounding the building, but from the outside she had not been able to see the receptionist or any on the twenty or so people milling around in the atrium. Jenny headed towards the reception and was surprised to see a look of shock appear on the girls face as she first looked up. The girl recovered her composure amazingly quickly and smiled as Jenny explained she was there to see Richard Pickles. 'I'm afraid I don't have you down on my list.' The girl smiled. 'Unfortunately Mr Pickles diary is very full and I can't let you through if you're not on my list. I'm very sorry. Perhaps you could try to ring through and set up an appointment for another time?'

'Sorry Analise, my mistake, I forgot to let you know Miss Cartwright was coming and she is a little late,' called a tall, slender man as he rushed down the stairs.

'No problems, Mr Pickles,' Analise coloured.

'Miss Cartwright. You only just caught me.'

Jenny followed Richard Pickles up the main staircase and into a glass lift which went up only one floor but then the doors opened on the opposite side into his inner sanctum.

'My girl's away today as I was only expecting to nip into the office, so it's a bit quiet around here.' Richard Pickles was tall and elegant but ebullient in the way he talked. He looked young, but the greying at his temples gave him a mature look that Jenny liked. His eyes glistened when he talked, he showed her through into his office and indicated for her to sit on a three piece suite near the door. The office was bigger than Jenny's flat and had a huge empty desk at the opposite end and a very modern espresso machine on the table along with a variety of other drinks and snacks behind the sofa

'May I ask what you have been up to this morning? Only you look a little dishevelled. I'm assuming it has something to do with why you're so late.' Richard Pickles smiled.

Jenny caught sight of her reflection in the glass panelling around the espresso machine.

'Oh my God, what do I look like? I am so sorry. I see why your receptionist didn't like the look of me now.' Jenny's face was covered in soot except for below her eyes where tears had cleared a stream down her face. Her white blouse was smoke stained and one sleeve was torn and the knees on her jeans were both ripped. 'I was involved in a fire last night. When Veronica said you were leaving the country I jumped straight into a taxi in the hope you wouldn't have left yet. I haven't looked in a mirror since yesterday.'

'Well it sounds like you've had one hell of a night. Why don't you pop in here and freshen up.' He opened a hidden door and showed her a private bathroom. 'There is a spare shirt in the cupboard over there and I will get us both a coffee whilst you sort yourself out. Don't rush we have plenty of time.'

Once Jenny had cleaned herself up she changed into Richard Pickles clean shirt and went back into the main office. He settled her down in one of the most comfortable chairs she had ever sat it and brought over a coffee.

'Better?'

'Yes much. Thank you.'

'Right, so Veronica tells me you have somehow got yourself involved in the Pharmcorp deal and you wanted to ask me some questions?' He had suddenly changed into a completely different person. The shutters had come down and his eyes had grown two shades darker. No more pleasantries, this was business.

'Yes Charlie left me some shares in his will. We were old friends,' she blushed. She didn't know why she did that, she had never been embarrassed by her job, but she didn't want him to judge her. 'I need to vote at the board meeting over whether to sell Pharmcorp to Bensons. I have read through the contract and the briefing notes and I have spoken to Terry St John and Vicki Swansen but I wanted an independent view.'

'What does it matter? If the sale goes ahead you will be a very rich woman. Why do you need all this information?' Richard was very stern and seemed confused by her need to talk.

'Charlie gave me these shares because he trusted me to do the right thing, and not just to leave me lots of money. As far as I can see my options are to save everyone's jobs but at the risk of Pharmcorp not being able to develop the drug, or sell and get the drug developed but there is no guarantee of the staff keeping their jobs. Only it isn't even that simple. There are issues of future development of the drug too.'

'Wow you have done your research.' Richard said. 'So why do you need me?'

'Well if this drug is so great and the potential is so massive, why did you pull out of the sale?'

'Good point. I can't give you all the details but the potential of the drug is massive, if it works.'

'Surely it must work otherwise why would Bensons be prepared to spend so much on buying it? '

'Well there is a lot of money in perception. Nothing cures the common cold and yet the business of selling cold remedies is worth billions. If people thought one company had the cure they would only buy from them. People don't really know when a cold is cured and a bit of paracetomol does wonders to clear you head.'

'So you're saying you pulled out because the drug doesn't work.'

'No I'm saying I looked into it because I was an old friend of Charlie's but I just wasn't convinced that the drug really worked. There are a lot more clinical trials that need to be done. If I'm wrong that decision has cost me billions, but to run those trials I would have had to spend millions. We aren't as big as Bensons and I can't afford to throw millions after a maybe. They can.'

Richard drank from his coffee and sat silently for a moment.

'Look it sounds to me like your biggest concern is for

the staff. You could give them a share issue before the buyout. If you split your shares one percent to the staff and keep six percent, you would still be very rich and they would all walk away with about a million each, that's got to make up for the possibility of them losing their jobs. And they may keep their jobs.'
'Thanks that starts to make a bit more sense now.'
'No problems but I am afraid I need to leave now. I will get my chauffeur to drop you home.'
'Thank you and what about your shirt?'
'Save it until we meet again.' Richard smiled and headed for the exit as another man entered and offered to take Jenny home.

Chapter eleven – Finding Mike

Jenny felt a little self conscious as she was dropped off outside the flats in Richard Pickle's chauffeur driven limousine. She rushed in for a well earned shower and some sleep. After the shower she wrapped herself in her fleeciest pyjamas, made herself a large milky hot chocolate and settled down on the sofa to watch Love Actually and try to switch off her brain. Everything was very confused and she was still no closer to a decision. She was woken later by the telephone. It was Terry St John.

'Hi Jenny, how are you?' he smarmed.

'Fine thanks Terry. It's been a tough couple of days so I was just catching up on some sleep'

'Sorry I didn't realise. Is there anything I can do to help?'

'Not really I just needed to get some sleep, to try and get my head straight.'

'Well I was surprised you didn't call. I thought I would be able to help you understand the deal.'

'Actually Terry that might be really helpful. Are you free later today?'

'Sure am. How about dinner at Punchinello's? I have a feeling you could do with a treat.'

'That would be lovely. See you there about seven?'

Jenny loved Punchinello's. It was set in a 16th century building and was very secluded with little cubbyholes for individual tables all over the place. She always felt sorry for the waiters who not only had to contend with the strange set up but also had to cope with the uneven floors such an old building offered.

Terry was already waiting for her when she arrived and greeted her with a kiss on each cheek. They ordered a selection of antipasti to start, followed by gnocchi in a gorgonzola sauce for Jenny and sword fish steak with asparagus and sautéed potatoes for Terry. Jenny was really enjoying the meal and no mention of the buyout had been made. She realised now why people liked Terry St John, and how he had charmed the women on the board before.

After main course, Jenny excused herself and as she was precariously making her way to the toilet she spotted Jet Smythe. He was whispering to someone but she couldn't quite work out who it was.

On leaving the bathroom Jenny took at slightly different route back to her table to try to see who Jet was talking to, but whoever it was, was no longer there. She returned to the table to find Terry in animated conversation with Veronica Smythe.

'You know I can't side with you over Vicki. She would never forgive me. She's determined to run this company and prove to everyone she's as good as her father.' Veronica whispered.

'But you know the deal is for the best. Think of what she could do with the money.' Terry looked up in time to see Jenny walking towards them.

'Ah Jenny, I believe you've met Veronica Smythe.'

"Yes Veronica, how are you?'

'More importantly how are you dear. After everything that's happened I suppose you must be wondering what is going on.' Veronica put her hand on Jenny's shoulder.

'Fine thank you. It's been great to enjoy some good company without worrying about everything that's been going on recently.'

'Yes. Did you get chance to talk to Richard this afternoon?'

'Thank you for that. He was very helpful.'

'Well I must return to Jet he will be wondering what's happened to me.' Veronica smiled and walked backed towards the table where Jenny had seen Jet earlier.

Jenny sat down and smiled at Terry once more.

'I suppose we do need to talk about the buyout.'

'Not at all dear. Let's order desert and then I can answer any questions you have.'

'I do have one before desert. Who's Veronica with?'

Jenny knew it was Jet but she didn't want Terry to know

she had seen him around.

'Oh that's Jet Smythe, her son from her second marriage
to Peter Smythe. I'm surprised to see him here, he's
usually only to be found in sleazy night clubs
frequented by drug dealers and strippers. No offence.'

'Not all night clubs have both strippers and drug dealers

you know,' Jenny said. 'Mike has a strict no drugs

policy and, is the reason some of the girls managed to

get clean.'

'Sorry. I guess I had an image of a seedy nightclub in

my mind, which I going to have the change now I've

met you.'

'Oh don't be sorry. Our club is clean but it doesn't mean

they all are.' Jenny smiled.

After enjoying one of the best tiramisus she had ever
tasted, they settled down to enjoy a coffee and a brandy.
Jenny's mind turned to the buyout.

'So I guess you are keen for the buyout to go ahead?'

'I am, but not necessarily for the reasons you think. Charlie and I built the business up from nothing and I am now ready to retire and reap the benefits of my labours, but I don't want everything it stood for to be lost. The work we have carried out over the years has been ground breaking and there is so much more the lab could do, but not without a serious influx of cash and equipment.' Terry was obviously very passionate about the business and did seem to be thinking about more than just the money.

'And what about the staff?' Jenny looked at him to check his reaction.

'There is a clause in the deal that states all staff will be given 0.005% of the purchase price whether they are kept in a job or not. If the sale goes through as expected they should get around two hundred and fifty thousand pounds each. Now most of them have been with us since the start, so that would be a very nice boost to their retirement. Anyone who wants to should be able to move into a job with Bensons, based on them being immensely qualified in their field.' Terry smiled over the top of his brandy glass and savoured the aroma as he drank.

'Wow, definitely sound like this is the right thing to do but aren't you afraid that the development will be lost and that Bensons will just milk it for everything they can.'

'I see you have been doing your homework. When the patent runs out, Bensons will need something to replace it so they will want to continue the development to ensure their next revenue stream. Bensons have an awful lot of government contracts, they have more chance than anyone to do the things Vicki wants to achieve. She is just trying to prove she can do more with this company than Charlie did. Which is admirable, but maybe she should just start afresh, and not live in Charlie's shadow.'

That evening, as Jenny was settling down to sleep, she thought she had made her mind up about the buyout, but the thing keeping her awake now was why Veronica's son had been arguing with Mike at the club a few days before. She was fairly sure he was the man who knocked Mindy over and she couldn't work out how Mike and Jet could possibly be linked and what if anything it had to do with the Pharmcorp buyout. Could it really be a coincidence? She resolved the only thing to do was to find Mike, and she had a feeling she knew where to look for him.

The next morning Jenny dug out the contract and checked Terry's point about the payment for staff. He was right, it was there in black and white. She was now sure the best thing to do was to agree to the buyout, but she wasn't going to show her hand before the board meeting just in case anything else came to light that made her change her mind.

The next thing was to track down Mike. She jumped onto the first train out of Nottingham and headed over to Beeston. She had this strange feeling she was being followed and she didn't want to draw any trouble to Mike. She looked around the train, looking for a face she recognised but couldn't see one. When she got off the train at Beeston station, she went in the opposite direction to the one she had planned, and doubled back through some of the side streets. All the time she kept looking around, and occasionally stopping and trying to look at reflections in shop windows. After twenty minutes of not getting anywhere, she realised that she was more spooked by what had been going on that she thought, and resolved to stop being so paranoid.

She could have sworn the strange little man who had been in Skegness was at Nottingham Station, but there had been no sign of him since. Nottingham rugby team had a match that afternoon and as far as she knew Mike had never missed one. Checking out the Victoria Inn where he usually enjoyed a pint, she was disappointed when there was no sign of him. She walked down to the ground and bought a ticket, wandering around trying to spot him, but no luck. Just as she was thinking she had made a mistake, she noticed a man heavily wrapped up against the cold standing by the burger stand. There was something about the way he stood that made her look twice. It was Mike. Jenny ambled over and ordered a burger and whilst she stood waiting for it to be cooked, sidled up to the man she thought was Mike.

'Thought I might find you here,' she smiled and spoke out of the side of her mouth while watching the game.

'Don't look at me. It's important no-one knows where I am.'

'Now the club's gone, there's not much else they can do is there?'

'They've said they hurt some of you girls. I could believe it when I heard that you and Blossom were in hospital. How is she?'

'She's in a bad way, but she'll pull through. What about you?'

'I need to wait for the insurance to come through, and then I can pay them off. I won't be able to rebuild the club but at least they will be off my back.'

'Who are they Mike? And how did you get into this mess?'

'Local thugs. I refused to let them deal drugs in my club. They said the only way to stop them was to pay protection. They knew a few secrets about my past which would have caused problems with my licence, and a couple of the girls don't need their pasts catching up with them so I agreed. Problem was when the club hit hard times, I wasn't making enough to cover all the bills and pay them.'

'And what does Jet Smythe have to do with all this?'

'How do you know about Jet Smythe?'

'I saw him arguing with you in the club and I'm fairly sure he was the bloke who knocked Mindy over coming out of the club on the day of the fire.'

'He's hired muscle for the gang. He's not up to much, but he's an evil little fucker and keen to twist the knife where he can. I think he's probably paying off some debt to them, by doing their dirty work but I don't know.'

'Well he's also Charlie's ex wife's son so he shouldn't be short of a bob or two.'

Jenny took her burger from the vendor and turned to Mike.

'Mike how much do you owe?'

'With interest it's fifty thousand.'

'Right get to mine tomorrow and we'll get this sorted once and for all. You can sell me the club and then we'll

see if they try it on with me. My background is very murky but I don't care who knows and there's nothing to stop me getting a licence and running the club.'
'But the club's been gutted.'
'Nothing that can't be rebuilt. It needed an upgrade anyway. Til tomorrow.'

As Jenny was getting off the train back in Nottingham it was starting to get dark. She was feeling much more confident, now she had found Mike and made a decision on the buyout. Everything was going to work out for the best. As she strolled along King's Walk, she thought she heard someone behind her. She glanced back but there was no-one there. Continuing along the road, there where light footsteps running up behind her. As she turned, something glinted in the streetlight, and a strange numbing sensation started to spread across her arm. The youth was wearing a grey hoodie and stood at about six feet tall. Her grabbed her bag and started to run. All the times she had told women that you should let go of the bag and never put yourself in danger, and here she was hanging onto the bag. Fighting with him. 'Let go you bitch.' the thief shouted and swung hitting her in the face with her own handbag.. Her vision swam and she was starting to black out.

'Help, help, someone help.' She called as she fell to the floor. The youth started to kick her and she rolled into the foetal position desperately trying to protect her head. He landed two very sturdy kicks to her ribs, before running away. Just as she lost consciousness she had a feeling of someone else running up the road towards her. Not again, she thought and the rest was black.

Chapter twelve – Confronting Veronica

'Jenny, Jenny, it's me Carly, try and open your eyes,'
Carly's gentle voice seemed to be floating above
whatever fog Jenny was sitting in the middle of. Jenny
blinked. The fog got brighter, almost too bright to see.
She winced, squinted and carefully tried to open her
eyes again.

'Nurse, I think she's waking up.' Carly called.

A shadow passed through the bright fog of Jenny's

vision and lifted her arm. A cool hand gripped her wrist.

'Pulse is strong. That's good,' said a gruff man's voice

Jenny didn't recognise.

 Jenny blinked and then tried to open her eyes fully. The
light seemed unnaturally bright but the more she
blinked the softer things became. She was looking up at
a ceiling of polystyrene tiles with fluorescent lights
hanging from them. A door closed softly and she tried
to call out, afraid she was alone in this alien
environment. As she tried to speak a croak emitted from
her dry throat. Carly's face appeared in her eye line.

'The doctor's on his way to check you over. Try not to move for a little while longer.' Jenny could just make out Carly's red eyes. Had she been crying?

The doctor arrived a few minutes later and checked Jenny's pulse. He shone a light in her eyes, she winced and closed her eyes.

'Come on now Miss Cartwright. I know this hurts but I need to check you out,' the doctor said.

Jenny opened her eyes and concentrated upon the wall behind him, trying to block out the pain as he poked and prodded her.

'You look like you've been a very lucky lady.' he smiled ' Nothing that won't heal but you will need to stay here for a few days. And then home to complete rest. The police will want to speak to you at some point.' He patted her hand. 'Don't worry; I will let them know you're too weak to talk now. Carly here can make you comfortable and then I am sure we can let you see a few visitors.'

The doctor closed the door behind him and Carly arranged the bed and her pillows so Jenny could sit up and look around. She was in a single room that didn't look like anything she had seen in hospital before.

121

Pastel shades on the walls, a large TV and a telephone. She could just make out through the door to her left, what looked like a private bathroom. She looked at Carly and raised an eyebrow, still not sure if her voice would work.

'Private room organised by Richard Pickles himself, no less. You obviously made an impression there.' Carly said. 'Let me get you some water.'

Carly fetched a glass and Jenny drank slowly. The cool cold water lubricating her throat and getting rid of the arid taste she had had since waking.

'What happen anyway? If that guy hadn't appeared when he did, things could have been a lot worse for you.'

'I don't know,' Jenny said. 'I was just walking home when this guy ran up to me. He must have had a knife, because I can remember there was blood on my arm before he even grabbed for my bag. I don't know why I didn't let him have the bag, there was nothing in it, but I hung on. Even when he'd got the bag he started kicking me, I thought he would have run but he just kept kicking me. That's all I can remember.' Jenny took a large gulp of water, talking even for a short while, hurt.

'Well luckily, Mr Parker came along in the nick of time and scared him off. He called the ambulance and stayed with you until they came.' Carly said. 'Is this linked to Charlie's death?'

'Why should it be?'

'Well he stabbed you before he even went for the bag and then he stayed to get a few kicks in. It all sounds a bit personal to me.'

'But why attack me? This is all about Mike and the club, nothing to do with me.'

'Come on Jenny, you've been the target twice now and you were at the club when the fire started.'

'I don't … I mean surely this isn't about me. Is it?' Jenny looked up at the ceiling trying to gather her thoughts. 'Well at least we know the fire wasn't meant for me.'

'Do we?'

'Well I'm fairly sure that was to do with blackmailing Mike and if I'm right we need to talk to Veronica's son Jet.'

'So you think Jet started the fire, and you still think this has nothing to do with Charlie's death. I think you're fooling yourself.'

'Maybe I am but I'll know more, once I've spoken to him.' Jenny moved to get comfortable and winced. There was a large bandage on her arm and as she pushed aside her pyjama jacket she could see her middle was covered in bruises. 'Exactly how bad am I?'

'Two broken ribs and a superficial cut on your left arm. Doctor says you were lucky he didn't get a kick into your head.'

Jenny looked around the room some more. There were a large number of cards and bouquets of flowers on most of the flat surfaces around the room.

'Where have all these come from?'

'Well there are ones from Me, Mindy and Blossom but they looked small beer once all the others turned up. Veronica, Vicki and Terry have all sent you a bouquet but the biggest one over there is from Richard Pickles. What happened with him? He seems to have taken a shine to you.'

'He was really kind and helped me to make a decision. He's a real gent. Oh no.'

'What?'

'I just realised I was still wearing his shirt when I was attacked. I was going to wash it and send it back, but I'll have to get him a new one now. I don't think you can pick a shirt like that up in Burtons.'

'Hang on a minute why were you wearing his shirt?'

Jenny told Carly about her meeting with Richard Pickles that morning.

'Sounds like a nice guy.' Carly smiled. "bout time you had someone interesting in your life.'

'I hardly think so, the guys is a multi millionaire who runs his own company. I don't think an over the hill stripper is going to be his idea of girlfriend material. Do you?'

'Based on the strings he pulled to get you this room, and the flowers, I think he might not have the same prejudices you have. Anyway, I'll leave you to get some rest and come back with the girls later on. Blossom is due to be released today, so we can set you both up in an invalid's home once you are ready to come out. The Carly Summers' Home For Convalescing Strippers, has a ring to it don't you think?'

Jenny was starting to feel more like her old self by the afternoon and was rudely reminded of her tender state, by the pain in her arm and her ribs every time she moved. She refused pain killers, wanting to keep her head straight to try to sort things out. The day she was attacked, she had phoned Terry St John to tell him she had read the contract and that she had to find a friend.

He might have known it was Mike she was looking for,
but there was no way he knew where she was going.
She had felt like she was being followed right from the
point she got on the train. Had the attack been just a
random bag snatch, or was it personal like Carly said?

That evening Jenny enjoyed having the girls sitting
around her bed and chatting about old times. Blossom
was going to move in with Mindy, while she
recuperated and Carly was busy with her studies, as
there was no work at the moment. Mindy had decided to
go and try out one of the other clubs in town. She
couldn't wait for Mike to turn up and decide what he
was doing with the club, she needed the money. Jenny
offered to cover their rents while they found other work,
but they wouldn't hear of it. They would manage
somehow, they just weren't sure how at the moment.
Once the bell rang for the end of visiting they all
hugged each other, carefully in both Jenny and
Blossom's cases, and left for the night.

During the night Jenny woke to hear arguing outside her
door.
'Who do you think you are?' called the night nurse.
'Just a surprise visitor for Miss Cartwright, I couldn't
make it any earlier and I wanted to see her.' It was a

man's voice and it sounded apologetic. Jenny thought

there was something familiar about it, but she couldn't

be sure.

'Well there's no visiting at this time of night. I need you

to leave now, or I will have to call security.'

'Yes I understand. Can I give you a number for her to

call in the morning?'

'I'm not an answering service, even if she is in a private

room you know.'

'Please, it is important.'

'Fine. Give it here and I will try and remember, but I

have got other patients you know.'

'I understand. Thank you so much,' the voice sounded

desperate but Jenny was drifting in and out of sleep and

not even sure it wasn't a dream.

The next morning Jenny decided she might try to get to

the bottom of one of the mysteries that had been

troubling her. She rang Veronica Smythe and asked if

she would be free for a visit later that day. Veronica had

said she would love to visit but couldn't make it until

mid afternoon as she was tied up all morning with her

charity work. The rest of the day was spent uneventfully

until lunch arrived. The joys of private health care are

mainly to be found in the food. A starter of chicken

liver pate and toast, followed by roast chicken and finished with a lemon syllabub, all washed down with fresh grape juice. Jenny then had a visit from the doctor, who was impressed with her progress and had decided if everything was okay over night she would be sent home the next morning. Unfortunately the main thing with broken ribs was to let them heal themselves, and a hospital stay didn't necessarily increase the healing process, even if Richard Pickles was paying a premium for her room.

About three o clock in the afternoon, Veronica arrived looking as tailored as ever. A grey Chanel suit with the skirt falling to just below the knee and black patent court shoes, with a two inch heel, all topped off with a delicate gold crucifix and a small velvet clutch bag.

'Oh how wonderful to see you're on the mend.' Veronica said as she walked into the room. Jenny had decided to get back into bed, to try and milk the injury a little, and produce the desired effect for the questions she needed to ask.

'I am feeling much better thank you. The ribs are still a little painful and I was lucky he only scrapped my arm when he tried to stab me. Everyone here has been so kind and the flowers have really cheered me up.' Jenny wafted her hand towards the large number of bouquets still colourfully covering the window sill and cupboard tops around the room. 'If you don't mind me saying you are hardly dressed for charity work.'

'Oh I don't do the actual work dear. I am on the committee, we decide how to raise money and once it's raised the best way to spend it. We have other people who do the work.'

'Oh I see. What charity is it?'

'I used to be involved in quite a few, but I couldn't really dedicate enough time to them all so I just focus on one now. It's a drug rehabilitation centre out in the old Colwick Hall.'

'Yes. I have been over there a few times. I help battered women and sometimes, we have to get them into rehab to help them break away from their abuser. How did you get involved?'

'Oh you know. People just know you are active and they ask you to get involved. I felt it was a good cause.'

'So nothing to do with your son being in there then?'

Veronica flinched but only slightly and then smiled, 'I'm not sure what you mean, my son?'

'Yes Jet. Blossom recognised him when he came running out of the back of the club just before the fire started. You see that was the rehab Mike had put her into, and she was sure that was where she recognised him from.'

'Well Jet has had some problems in the past but he's sorted now. He has set himself up in business and he is doing very well. I haven't had to increase his allowance for a number of months.'

'And Jet has told you all about this business, has he?'

'No,' Veronica said. 'My son is a grown man, who

doesn't need to justify everything he does to me.'

'I'm sorry to tell you this Veronica but Jet's a hired

thug.'

'Don't be so stupid. Why would my baby want to do anything like that?' Veronica shouted.

'Calm down, just listen to what I have to say please.'

'Okay but your wrong. Charlie told me you were astute and kind, so I don't understand why you would say such horrible things. Haven't I been nice to you since Charlie's death?'

'Yes you have and that's why I have to tell you these things.' Jenny put her hand on Veronica's arm and started to fill her in on everything she knew.

Veronica paced around the room and listened carefully to everything Jenny had to say.

'No, no you're wrong. Why are you saying such things?

Turns out you are just a dirty little stripper after all. Charlie was wrong about you.' Veronica stormed out of the room. Jenny closed her eyes and tried to hold back the tears. She knew she was right and that Veronica was only protecting her son, but the insults she had thrown really hurt.

Later that evening the night nurse arrived and popped into Jenny's room with a business card.

'Sorry I forgot to give this to you when I left this morning. He was quite insistent that you got it.' The nurse handed over the card and on the front it said: Mr Jonathan Parker; Personal Security and Investigation Services, followed by a mobile phone number. Oh the back in very neat handwriting it read "Don't leave the safety of the hospital without calling me first".

So the dream from last night had been real after all and maybe the attack had not been a random mugging. Whoever Jonathan Parker was, he obviously thought she would be safe in hospital but she was being discharged in the morning. Could she trust him, or was this just a ruse to get her on her own? Wasn't Parker the name of the man who found her? Maybe he would have some answers. Jenny decided the best thing would be to sleep on it, and make a decision in the morning.

When Jenny woke her head was feeling clearer. She decided meeting Mr Parker would be the first thing she would do, when she was released. After all if he had meant her harm he could have sneaked back after she had gone to sleep the night before. He had sounded harmless enough when she had heard him in the corridor, but she wanted to check with one person before she made the phone call.

She eased herself out of bed and, slipping on a pair of hospital slippers, shuffled from her room to the nurses' station.

'Miss Cartwright I really don't think you should be out of bed,' said the nurse looking up from her notes.

'It's okay. I just needed to ask you a question.'

'Miss Cartwright,' the nurse raised an eyebrow.

'The gentleman who gave you this card, what was he like?'

Jenny showed the nurse the business card from Mr Parker. The nurse took the card and held in turning it over in his hand. She noticed the writing on the back.

'Well I wouldn't have given you the card if I had seen this,' she held the back of the card up for Jenny to see.

'Perhaps it's as well you did. Some strange things have been happening and I need to know if I can trust Mr Parker.'

'He seemed quite normal. He was a small man, for a man if you know what I mean and he was just well... non-descript.'

'And do you think he was dangerous?' Jenny asked thinking this Mr Parker sounded a little like someone she had met before.

'Oh no not at all. He was very apologetic that he was here so late. He almost begged me to give you the card. He didn't try to force it on me or even want to disturb you.'

'Thank you,' Jenny said.

'Now get back to bed, it's not even six thirty yet,' the nurse smiled and returned to her paperwork.

Jenny returned to her room and rang the number on the card. A public meeting would be safe enough she was sure. She agreed to meet Mr Parker in Holly's Café and promised to take a taxi, and not a private one at that. The rest of the morning was spent waiting for the doctor to do his final checks and discharge her.

She arrived at Holly's cafe feeling sore and settled herself down in one of the booths. Private enough for a conversation, but not so private that people wouldn't be able to see what was going on. She faced the door and ordered a bacon sandwich and a milky coffee both of which were brought to the table. She hadn't realised how bad she must have looked, until she got table service, apart from the bandages which were not obvious, she was sporting two fantastic black eyes and walking with a stick. Usually when she came in she was fully made up and immaculately dressed. Today's look was definitely shocking.

After about twenty minutes Jenny looked up to see the little man walk in. Upon closer inspection he was not that little, just little for a man. He must have been about five feet seven inches, which was the same height as Jenny without her heels. Blonde with grey alert eyes he constantly seemed to be looking around.

'Do you mind if I sit facing the door please.' He looked at Jenny and gave her the impression of one of those presidential protection officers, all that was missing was the ear piece.

'Not at all but you'll have to get in next to me. It took me all week to get sat down, I'm not moving unless I have to.' Jenny smiled.

He sidled in next to her and finally held out his hand for it to be shaken.

'I'm Jonathan Parker, Mr McGuffin asked me to keep an eye on you.'

'Pleased to meet you. I saw you at the seaside when the caravan was trashed didn't I?'

'Yes. Unfortunately I was so busy keeping an eye on you, I didn't see what happened to the caravan, but I have my suspicions.'

'Where you on the train when I went to Beeston.'

'Yes. I must apologise for that.'

'Why you got rid of him for me?'

'I was distracted at the station and lost you for a few minutes. I should have been there when he first went for you. That way we might have caught him, and he definitely wouldn't have had time to attack you.'

'And based on your calling card, you must still think I'm in danger.'

'I'm not sure. I can't yet work out how this all fits together. I know the attacker was Jet Smythe but I haven't been able to ascertain whether it is to do with Mike and the club or Charlie and the will.'

'Well you need to find out because if it's to do with Mike and the club the other girls could be in danger.'

'Mr McGuffin told me you were impressive,' He smiled. 'Not many women would have gone through what you've been through and have as their first thought, the safety of their friends.'

'I need to know they're not in any danger.'

'I will do my best to keep an eye on everything, but I can't watch all four of you.'

'Well then just watch Jet and hopefully that will protect us all. Mike and I will be sorting out the sale of the club in the next few days. Once that goes through there will be no need for Jet to try to frighten anyone. If it doesn't stop him we can look elsewhere for his motives. After all ex-druggies tend not to be that clever, so there must be a "Mr Big" behind what he is doing. Can you track him down?'

'I have tried but the only contact he has really had is with his mother.'

'I spoke to her yesterday about him, Let me try again, I think I was getting somewhere.'

'Okay but promise me you won't go alone.'

'I don't think Veronica Smythe is going to hurt me, do you?'

'No but she could tell Jet where you are.'

'I hardly think so.' Jenny shook her head.

'Veronica will only see the best in her son and if he says he wants to talk to you, she will set it up. You just need to be careful. Stop seeing the best in people, there are some evil bastards out there.'

'Okay I'll be careful. I have a friend, who I can ask to go with me,' Jenny smiled and before she knew it Jonathan Parker was gone.

Chapter thirteen – Family ties

Mindy was struggling for money, with the club out of action so she needed to find work. She went over to Derby and headed towards one of the clubs on Sadler Gate, where the owner knew Mike. The club was much more modern than the Blue Lagoon Gentleman's Club and had scantily clad dancers in cages on a Friday and Saturday night. As they weren't strippers, this appealed to both sexes and had earned the club the name of being the place to be.

The back door was open and Mindy walked in. Daylight did the room no favours. The floor was sticky and the black walls were covered in marks and stains. The stage was curtained off and only used on the very rare occasion the owner hired a band, and in front of it was the DJ stand. Either side of the stand were two metal cages for the dancers. Sometimes scantily clad boys were used but only if there was a promise of a couple of hen parties. There were four other cages scattered around the room about six feet off the ground and two others with glass bottoms about eight feet off the ground. As Mindy was taking all this in, the owner appeared from down the cellar.

'Well hello little lady, what can I do for you?' Jack Foster was forty years old, but looked much older. He was overweight and sweating. He was rubbing his hands together as he approached Mindy and she had a feeling her personal space was about to be invaded. His hair was thinning and swept across his head, held there by sweat. Mindy had heard the only reason anyone worked for him was that he paid well, but for that he wanted the best and they had to put up with his attention. He never forced himself on the women, he just liked to look. Rumour had it that he was still a virgin and he lived at home with his mum, but no-one was really sure.

'Oh. Hi there. I'm one of Mike Peter's girls and I was wondering if you had any work.' Mindy stammered. She didn't like Jack but she needed to find something and this was the best club around.

'We're not a strip club you know. This is a respectable establishment.'

'I never said it was.' She smiled her sweetest smile and wrinkled her nose. This helped in two ways, as it made her look extremely pretty and blocked some of the smell of old sweat, emanating from Jack's body. 'It's, just, I heard one of your girls left and you need someone quick. I can dance really well.'

'Well I could do with someone. Sonia went off and got herself married and her husband won't let her dance. Says it's not right for his wife. It was alright when he met her, but not now apparently.'

'I only need something temporary until Mike gets the club sorted. I could be a stand in while you look for someone else.'

'I tell you what, how about an audition.' He smiled. She assumed it was meant to be a smile, but it came over as a leer. Jack went and fetched a small step ladder and helped her into the cage. He walked over to the DJ stand and started some music. Mindy closed her mind to Jack watching her. She got into the rhythm and danced to three tracks before Jack turned off the music. He helped her down from the cage. She was sweating nearly as much as him.

'I'll give you a trial. Come back tonight, ten pm and we'll see how you get on.'

'Great thanks, I'll see you later.'

Mindy left the club, finally thinking things were starting to go her way.

That evening Mindy was enjoying her first night and she was turning into a sensation. A petit Asian woman who could easily turn upside down and hang precariously in the cage, she made the other dancers look like beginners. She had developed a bit of a crowd and was getting a fan base.

'Wow look at that beauty dance. She can dance round my pole any time, hey boys,' called an enthusiastic

Asian man who was surrounded by a group of his friends. The rest of the group turned round and started jeering and laughing. All big boys once they were out on the town, happy to act like big men, but Mindy knew they wouldn't be like that back home. Then they would be respectful boys, good to their mothers, and hopefully their wives.

'Lads, anyone going to help me?' a call from behind them made them all turn round as another member of their group appeared trying to carry six bottles of beer at once.

'Oh thanks, Dilip, what do you think of the babe in the cage?' Mindy looked over at the group at the same time as Dilip looked up at her. Time stopped. Dilip pushed past his friends and rushed to the cage.

'Must be love boys,' jeered the group leader.

'What are you doing there?' Dilip shouted as he reached the bottom of the cage.

'Trying to earn a living since I was disowned,' Mindy shouted back.

'Oi, I'm paying you to dance not chat.' Jack called from the side of the stage where he watched the show each night.

'I get off at three am, will you wait?' Mindy looked worried. She desperately wanted to talk to Dilip.

141

'Of course I will,' he smiled and wandered back to his friends.

'Wow, got a date Dilip?' asked his friend

'Hardly, and I think you should be more respectful to a man's sister.' The other boys looked at him and then looked at the floor and drank the rest of their beers in silence.

As the club was closing, Dilip appeared on the emptying dance floor and Mindy rushed out from the back to greet him. She flung her arms around him and gave him a huge hug. Dilip stood there stunned for a few seconds and then returned the hug, lifting her up and swinging her round.

'Oh my God. It's so good to see you,' he smiled.

'You too,' she was so relieved to hear him say that. She hadn't seen him since before she lost the baby. 'Let's get out of here. There is an all night café around the corner. We can get a coffee and talk some.'

They sat opposite each other in the café, and Mindy demolished the full English breakfast that Dilip paid for.

'Anyone would think you didn't eat,' He smiled.

'Actually to look at you I'm not sure you do.'

'One of the joys of dancing is that you can eat what you want and the weight stays off.' She wasn't sure how he would react to knowing her real job just yet so she thought she would stick with dancer. It wasn't a lie after all.

'So, how are you coping?' He asked.

'Not bad. It was tough at first, but I have some really good friends now, girls I work with, and we help each other.'

'What I don't understand is why you felt you had to leave. Surely it would have been better to stay and let mum and Sunil look after you once you lost the baby.'

'They obviously didn't tell you the full story.' She leant across the table and held his hand.

'Well I know you lost the baby, but Sunil was devastated and then you just walked out. I know these things are tough but you should have stood by your husband.'

'Dilip, I lost the baby because Sunil raped and beat me.' She looked deep into his eyes.

'The bastard, let me get hold of him.' He started to get up. Dilip looked around the café, clenching and unclenching his fists.

'Dilip, it's too late now.' Mindy grabbed his arm and

pulled him back down into his seat. 'I am fine I'm just

glad you know the truth at last.'

'Why didn't mum help you? She took Sunil in. He lived
with us for six months, even brought girlfriends round
and she cooked for him, treated him like her own son.'

'Mum knew Sunil was beating me. She said it must be
because I was too headstrong. She said I had to try to
become a better wife. Then when I lost the baby that
wasn't the worse thing. They had to do a hysterectomy
to save my life. Sunil was happy to take me back until

he found out I couldn't give him the son he so

desperately wanted. I think he saw it as a dint in his
masculinity.'

'I am so sorry, I never knew. You know I would have
come and found you.'

'I know. How weird that we have found each other?'

'Yes. I go into that club most weeks and I have never
seen you before, how come you were there tonight.'

'Well I usually work in Nottingham but there was a fire
at the club, so I just had to find some work quick. My
friend Blossom was hurt in the fire, so she can't work at

the moment. She's staying with me and we needed some

money. I came over this afternoon and Jack said I could start tonight.'

'Wow that's great. You looked like a good dancer only I'm not sure where you learnt to hang from those poles like that.'

Mindy swallowed, now she had found him again there was no need for secrets, 'Dilip, please don't be mad but I'm not really a dancer as such. I'm a stripper.'

Dilip looked at her with his mouth wide open, she thought he was going to have a go, or just walk out and then he just burst out laughing. 'Mum will have a heart attack if she finds out and the mighty Sunil will not be so happy to know his wife is a stripper. You aren't divorced yet are you?'

'No, but please don't let them know where I am. It took me a long time to get my confidence back after what he did to me. I don't think I could cope with seeing him again.'

'Don't worry your secret is safe with me.'

Dilip and Mindy sat talking for quite a few hours and then Mindy realised she needed to get the early train back for Blossom. Dilip walked her to the station and promised to go over and see her in Nottingham as soon as he could.

Mindy sat on the train smiling to herself. The last twenty four hours had been great, she had got a new job, she had found her brother and he wasn't upset with her. Things were definitely looking up.

Chapter fourteen – A Tour and a meal

Jenny had spent a few days resting and trying not to do too much, but the solitude of her small flat, and with all of her friends elsewhere, she was starting to go stir crazy. She was more than willing when Vicki rang her and invited her for a tour of the Pharmcorp labs.

A car arrived, and Jenny headed off to a business park. The car was waved through the main gate by security. She was then driven up to the Pharmcorp front door and greeted there by a small, fawning man who introduced himself as Jeremy, Vicki's assistant. He apologised for Vicki's absence, explaining she had been called into an important meeting and that he had been instructed to give Jenny the tour. He seemed to almost bow as he was talking. He wore a brown dogtooth print suit and wore his black hair slicked back. He peered at Jenny through thick rimmed spectacles.

'Miss Swansen will be free by the time we've finished the tour,' he said, as he opened the main door and pointed to a smaller door on the left. 'Can you go through there and get changed? I will meet you on the other side.'

'Get changed?'

'Yes, the facility is what is known as a clean facility, so

you need some protective clothing. In the changing

rooms are some lockers where you can leave your coat

and bag. There is an assistant who will make sure you

have everything you need.'

A young woman standing at a counter greeted Jenny.

'If you would like to leave your coat, bag and any

jewellery in one of the lockers please,' the woman said.

'I'm not sure I like leaving all my things lying around.'

'Don't worry they have a key which you can attach to

the inside of your lab coat. No one can disturb them.'

Once Jenny had securely stowed everything away, the

woman gave her a lab coat, a hair net and some plastic

overshoes.

Jenny emerged through a second door into a white room

just as Jeremy emerged from a similar door on the

opposite side of the corridor.

As the tour started Jeremy showed Jenny down a

corridor where lab coated men and women poured over

chemical beakers and jars.

'This is where all the science starts,' Jeremy said. 'The

chemists work on potential drugs which then go through

a series of clinical trials and tests before they are approved and made available to the public.'

'Are all the tests carried out here?' Jenny asked.

'Some, but the initial ones are contracted out. It's very expensive to test drugs when they are first invented and security needs to be very high, so we tend to just pay someone else to do it for us.'

They continued walking and headed through a set of double doors which led into a factory where a liquid was being pumped into a small tray with little holes in it. The trays went through a metal door, and when they came out the other end of the machine the trays were tipped up and hundreds of tablets spilled out onto a conveyor belt.

'This is where the drugs are turned into tablet form. There is another machine over there that puts the drugs into capsules.' Jeremy said.

'And what's that over there?' Jenny giggled as she pointed to what looked like a large cement mixer. 'Looks a little like a cement mixer doesn't it?' Jeremy said. 'That's how we apply the coating to the tablet that makes them easier to swallow.

'Right, let's head back to Ms Swansen, unless you have any questions.'

'No but thank you for the tour. It helps to be able to see what we do here,' Jenny said and smiled.

Once Jenny had discarded her protective covering and retrieved her belongs, Jeremy then led her up to Vicki's office. They walked through a suite, with a sitting room, kitchen and bedrooms all furnished for maximum comfort. He left her in Vicki's outer office promising she wouldn't be kept long.

After about ten minutes the door opened and five bespectacled men in lab coats emerged from the office with Vicki following closely behind.
'Thanks for that, guys. Hopefully we can get the last of those clinical trials finished this week.' Vicki smiled and then spotted Jenny. 'Hi Jenny, sorry to keep you waiting but it's always so busy around here. I hope Jeremy looked after you okay. Come in, come in.'
Vicki ushered Jenny into her office and Jenny noticed how functional it was. There was a desk with a laptop and file on it and a large conference table for meetings. There were no photographs, no pictures on the walls, and no flowers anywhere to be seen. Jenny thought that

Vicki was going to extremes to not be seen as a woman in a man's world.

'So how did you enjoy the tour? Good to get a chance to see the business you own part of?'

'Yes, it was great thank you. To tell you the truth, I was at a bit of a loose end so the invite was a welcome distraction.'

'I suppose you're still recuperating, are you? How do you fancy a coffee? I think I might be able to rustle up some lunch, if you'd like to stay?'

'That sounds great, thank you.' Jenny said as Vicki wandered over to the telephone and barked some instructions. A few minutes later, Jeremy arrived with two cups of coffee and a plate of sandwiches. He laid the food and drinks on the conference table and left the room without looking at Vicki. The coffee was definitely not the type she had received when she visited Richard Pickles offices, but she sipped at it politely. It was awful, but she couldn't refuse it now Vicki had gone to the trouble to get lunch.

Over lunch, they chatted about the business and Vicki's plans for the growth of Pharmcorp. Jenny asked about the house she had walked through to get to Vicki's office.

'That's the accommodation suite. It's for the clinical

trials.' Vicki smiled.

'I thought Jeremy said they were carried out elsewhere.'

'Yes, the initial ones are, but in the end we have to test

on people, and we do that here in a controlled

environment. We know the drugs are safe and we are

happy they do what they should, but you can't get

clearance to sell something until you have proved they

work on people and the only way to do that is through

testing. We mainly use students, and it pays really well.'

Vicki took a sip of her coffee before she continued.

'There are some risks. I am sure you remember the case

a few years back where someone died and other people

were left seriously ill, but we have lots of checks in

place to make sure that doesn't happen.'

'Wow, it all sounds very exciting.'

'It is. At university, I studied literature, but I am really

enjoying working in the chemical world.'

'So you weren't disappointed that your father didn't

leave you the publishing house?'

'It would have been a dream come true for me, but he

needed me here, so I'll carry on with the work he

started.'

Jenny set her coffee cup down and leaned forward, 'Vicki, can I ask you a delicate question?'

'That sounds ominous. I suppose the worst I can do is throw you out.' She laughed. 'Don't be nervous, ask away.'

'How close are you to your half brother?'

Vicki's face dropped. 'Why do you ask?'

'It's just I have reason to believe he's responsible for the club burning down and he might have been the one who attacked me.' Jenny looked at Vicki carefully, half expecting her to explode and throw her out.

'To tell you the truth, I'm not surprised. He has never been any good since his father died. Before that really, but he definitely used his father's death as an excuse to go off the rails. The only person who still sees any good in him is my mother. But I suppose that is what mothers do. Isn't it?'

'I know what you mean. I tried to talk to Veronica but she wasn't interested in listening to what I had to say.'

'You've met Richard Pickles, haven't you?'

'Yes.'

'He was there when Pete Smythe died. Talk to him and see if the two of you can't talk some sense into my mother.'

153

'Sounds like a good idea but Richard is out of the
country at the moment, so I guess I'll have to wait.'
'Not anymore. Apparently the deal fell through and he's
come back early. Obviously, didn't want to lap up the
Caribbean sun. Prefers to be working I guess.'
'Thanks for that Vicki. You've been a big help.'
'No worries. And if Mum still won't talk to you let me
know, and I'll see if I can help.

Jenny was disappointed that Richard Pickles had not
contacted her, to let her know he was back in the
country. She definitely felt a connection when they met.
After all, he had organised the private room and sent her
those wonderful flowers. But he was the Chief
Executive Officer of a multi million pound operation
and she was a stripper. She had been involved in the
business world for less than a month and here she was
thinking she was something special, but she was still a
stripper, and she still lived in a tiny flat in a dodgy area
in the centre of Nottingham. Maybe he had just felt
sorry for her and forgotten that she could afford her own
private room.
She needed to stop thinking she was something special
and sort out things she had some control over. She had
to track down Mike and finalise the sale of the club,
then she could start rebuilding and get the girls back to

work. She was annoyed that Mike hadn't been in touch after she had tracked him down and told him she was ready to buy the club. He was supposed to be in a rush to sell and now he had vanished again. Mike would appear again soon, after all it was in his interest to finalise the sale.

She needed to find Jet and it looked like the most obvious route would be through Richard Pickles. Time to swallow her pride; he had after all given her his personal number so he shouldn't be upset if she called. Plus no matter what he thought about her, she needed to protect her friends. She settled down and found his business card and dialled the number.

'Hello, Richard Pickles speaking.'

'Hi Richard, its Jenny here, Jenny Cartwright. We met last week.' She was sure he wouldn't remember her, and even if he did, he wouldn't have time for her little problems.

'Hi Jenny, of course I remember you. I am so glad you called. I got back into the UK late last night and I was wondering when would be a good time to call.'

'You did?' Jenny enjoyed the welcoming tone of his voice.

'Yes. How are your injuries? Healing okay, I hope.'

'Definitely. Helped by the extra special care I got at the hospital,' she smiled, was she flirting with him after she had already decided he wouldn't be interested?

'I am glad. Listen I am sorry to rush you, but I am about to go into a meeting and whilst I would love to talk to you I can't at this precise moment.'

'Well I did want to ask you a big favour but it can wait.' She was sure he was only being polite.

'How about dinner tonight? Will it wait until then?'

'Yes.'

'Excellent I'll send a car for you and we can eat at the Raymond Blanc place on Thane Road. How about seven?'

'Fantastic. Thanks.' Jenny put down the phone and sat on the sofa with a silly grin on her face for the next few minutes. Then the panic set in. What was she going to wear for a meal at Raymond Blanc's? Time to spend a little of her new found wealth. She rang Blossom to see if she could do her make-up and headed into town to find a dress worthy of the best restaurant in town. Blossom was pleased to have a visitor, and even more excited that she was the first of the girls to know about the date. She checked out Jenny's little black dress and nodded approvingly. It had a good high neckline and a skirt that settled half way down her thighs, it was subtle and not too tarty. She wanted to dispel any preconceived notion he may have over how a stripper dressed. Blossom plaited Jenny's hair so she looked like Bo Derek in the movie Ten. Blossom was convinced that every man of a certain age lusted after Bo Derek in that movie and Richard Pickles was certainly of that age. She then gave Jenny a makeover. Strange how it took so long to do make-up, that looked like you weren't wearing any. Jenny left Mindy and Blossom's flat with over an hour to get across town and into her dress and a pair of five inch Jimmy Choo's. Richard was tall, so she knew the heels wouldn't over-power him.

The car arrived at seven pm exactly, and the chauffeur telephoned her to come down as he didn't feel comfortable leaving the vehicle outside the flats, while he collected her. As Jenny exited the building, the liveried chauffeur opened the rear door for her and ensured she was comfortable before pulling away into the hectic Nottingham traffic. She had expected the music to be classical and for the car to glide through the traffic almost as if it was not even in contact with the tarmac. She was pleasantly surprised to find the stereo playing Dock of the Bay by Otis Redding.
'The boss left you a note in the pull out section behind the front seat, madam.' The chauffeur called and then

closed the partition glass. Jenny carefully pulled down the opening to find a small bottle of Champagne and a crystal glass with a note.

To my favourite Pharmcorp board member, please enjoy the Champagne (I hope I chose right here) and the music (ditto) and I shall see you very soon. Don't be nervous. You will be the classiest lady in the joint. Richard.

Jenny smiled to herself and carefully opened the bottle. She poured it out, and sank back into the very comfortable seats, enjoying the music and the opulence. She arrived at the restaurant, and as the driver opened the door to let her out, Richard appeared.

'Let me help you.' He smiled, as he held out his hand to help her from the car. She had judged the heels perfectly and was just a few inches shorter that he was. They walked into the restaurant together and every head turned.

'Wow, that never happens when I eat here alone,' he said. He pushed her chair back in as they were seated. 'You look amazing, very Bo Derek.'

'Strangely enough, that was the effect my dresser was going for,' she giggled, not mentioning said dresser was Blossom.

Once they were settled, a waiter came out and poured a glass of Barolo for them. When Jenny tasted it she understood why the wine she usually drank was five pounds a bottle. The difference was incredible. Savouring the wine she looked for the menus, but there weren't any. Had Richard already ordered? It was sweet, but it did seem a little draconian and he didn't know what she didn't like. Suddenly a man in his fifties wearing chef's scrubs, whom Jenny had a strange feeling she recognised, walked over to the table.

'Ah Richard, how are you?' the chef smiled

'Good, thank you Raymond. May I introduce Jenny to you? She's a new board member at Pharmcorp. Jenny, Raymond, Raymond, Jenny.'

Jenny shook hands with the chef, 'Oh my god you are Raymond Blanc aren't you?' She blushed, ashamed she was coming across as a peasant, this probably happened all the time in these sorts of restaurants.

'Please don't be embarrassed, my dear. Richard told me he had a young lady to impress this evening so I offered to cook.' He smiled and bent to kiss the back of her hand. Jenny looked across at Richard who himself was now looking a little embarrassed.

'So, if you will allow me I would like to cook you a number of small courses showcasing my exceptional talents.' Jenny was too shell shocked to answer and when both of them smiled and nodded, Raymond backed away from the table, off to create something wonderful.

Jenny couldn't decide whether to ask her favour before the meal and risk spoiling the evening or after the meal and risk coming across as ungrateful.

'What's wrong, you seem distracted?' Richard asked.

'Did you not want to ask me a favour?'

'Yes, I did but I don't want to spoil the meal, if you feel I am asking too much.'

'Well, I tell you what, I promise not to get upset by the question, if you promise not to get upset by the answer. And whatever the question or answer is, once it has been asked and answered, whatever the outcome, we will forget about it and enjoy the meal.'

'Sounds like a plan.' Jenny smiled she still couldn't believe she was in such a fancy restaurant, sat across from such an attractive man. She swallowed hard, took a sip of her wine, and started. 'The thing is, you know Veronica Smythe quite well don't you?'

'Well I did. I hadn't spoken to her since her husband's funeral until she rang about you last week.'

'I think her son Jet is responsible for some bad things that have been happening to me and my friends, and I need Veronica's help to stop him.'

'Have you spoken to Veronica?'

'Yes. She visited me in hospital but she wouldn't listen to anything I had to say. My boss owes some money, protection money. I think that was the reason for the fire at the club. My friend Blossom was hurt in the fire. But she saw Jet leaving before the fire started. I think he is working for the people Mike owes money too. I also think Jet might have been the one that mugged me. I didn't tell Veronica that, I have no proof. I spoke to Vicki Swansen and she said you might be able to talk to Veronica and make her see he's not the angel she thinks he is.'

'I think this probably all stems back to his childhood and the way Veronica always spoilt him. He only had to sulk and she would cave in. Pete was stricter with him, but he was never there and then after he died, Veronica did everything she could to make sure Jet didn't feel he was missing out by not having a father. I know what he's capable of, and I am not surprised he hurts people, but why do you think he would have attacked you?'

'I don't know. I had offered to buy the club, so Mike would have been able to pay off his debts, but then the income would have stopped because I wouldn't be blackmailed. I am worried this all has something to do with Charlie's death but I don't know how or why.'

161

'Okay, I can see you're worried so why don't we both go and see Veronica tomorrow. Will that help?'

'It will. Hopefully she can help me find out why Jet is doing this and see if we can stop him.'

The first course turned up and the rest of the evening was spent enjoying some fantastic food. Richard rode back in the car with Jenny and as they arrived at the flats he leaned over and gave her a chaste kiss on the cheek.

'Until tomorrow,' He smiled and was gone.

Chapter fifteen – Convincing Veronica

The door bell rang and Jenny opened it to find the corridor empty. She step out of her flat and looked up and down the hallway but there was no one there. She turned and was about to re-enter when she heard voices.

'That's not a problem Mrs Jones. As long as you're okay.'

'Yes thank you. So nice to have a young man to help me. Jenny usually does but she's not been so good lately.'

'Mrs Jones, are you okay?' Jenny called heading towards her neighbour's open door.

'Oops looks like I should get on.' Richard appeared at the door.

'Well next time you must stop for some cake and tea.' Mrs Jones called after him.

Richard grabbed Jenny's hand and pulled her back into her flat, softly closing the door behind them.

'Thank you. I thought I'd never get away.' Richard said.

'What were you doing with Mrs Jones?'

'I heard her struggling from the lift with her shopping just after I rang your bell. I went to help and before I knew it we were in the kitchen and she was trying to force feed me Victoria sponge and brewing the biggest pot of tea.'

'Well you are a good looking man and we don't get many of them wandering around these flats.'

'Well hopefully I'll be wandering around these flats a lot more. Just to keep Mrs Jones happy, you understand.'

'Of course.' Jenny giggled as she blushed. 'I assume you're here for more than helping the little old ladies unpack there shopping.'

'Yes. Veronica has said she can see us this afternoon so I thought I would pick you up and we could have some lunch and then go and see her.'

'Sounds great. Only why don't we have some of Mrs Jones cake instead and then we can go?'

'If you want to take the risk of losing me before you've

even got me… lead the way.'

They arrived at Veronica's and were shown into the
drawing room by an old fashioned butler who brought
in a tray of tea and told them that madam had asked
they help themselves, as she had been delayed for a few
moments.

'I don't think, I've ever drunk so much tea. At least she

didn't put out any cake.' Richard said as he poured them

both a cup.
Jenny giggled and was sipping her tea as Veronica
swept into the room and rushed up to Richard kissing
him on both cheeks.
'How wonderful to see you,' she gushed. 'It has been too
long.'
'Yes it has. How have you been?'
'Good, thanks. It's been tough since Charlie died, but
you get on with it don't you,' she then turned and
noticed Jenny. 'Ahh I see you have been duped into
coming to talk to me about my supposedly wayward
son.'
'Veronica, I think you need to listen to what Jenny has
to say.' Richard said.

'Veronica, I didn't come here to cause you any problems. I just want to protect my friends and I think that Jet is trying to hurt them.' Jenny put her cup on the table and started to stand. Noticing Richard shake his head, she sat again.

'I know you are wrong, but if it will stop you from trying to persecute my son I will listen to your story. After that I don't want to hear anymore about it. Agreed?' Veronica sat next to Richard, facing Jenny. Jenny sat and explained in detail all the things that had been happening to her and her friends and why she thought Jet was to blame.

'So you have no proof?' Veronica asked after Jenny had finished talking.

'I know Jet was blackmailing Mike, but you are right I have no proof about the other attacks. It just seems strange that there are two people out to get us.'

Veronica's lowered herself to the sofa and rested her head in her hands. Jenny looked over at Richard not really sure what to do. Richard put his arm round Veronica's shoulder.

'I think it's time you admitted what you've known all along.' Richard spoke slowly and gently to Veronica and she lifted her head and nodded.

'You're right Jenny, Jet has never been the perfect son but I thought I could change him. After his father died we found out he had a drug problem, it took a long time for him to admit it and get help. I thought he was cured and I don't think he has gone back to the drugs, but he has probably switched one addiction to another, that of power.'

'Tell her everything Veronica.' Richard said. 'Jenny wants to help.'

'When Pete died we were all on a skiing holiday. There was me and Pete, Jet, Vicki, Richard and a few other people. As with most skiing holidays, people split up during the day and get back together in the evening. On the day of the accident Pete, Jet and Richard went off together to ski a black run. Jet had been in a strange mood, almost pensive, which was unusual for him and I don't think he really wanted to go. Maybe you should take up the story from here Richard.' Veronica wiped away the tears and turned to Richard, nodding very slightly.

'We had skied that particular black run many times, but there had been a slight dusting of snow which can make things worse, it hides dangers. The first run was fine, everyone got down without any problems and the added excitement of it being a little bit harder than the day before had got the adrenaline flowing. On the way back

167

up Jet and Pete shared a chair lift. I had got talking to one of the ski guides and followed them up probably about five minutes later. By the time I got to the top they were having a massive argument and all I heard was Pete shouting "I'm not bailing you out again" and shooting off down the ski run. Jet went after his father. I thought about leaving them to it, but the look in Jet's eyes convinced me to follow. By the time I found them Pete was unconscious, in the trees and Jet was standing over his father. Now I don't know how the accident happened but I do know that Pete was too good a skier to have gone near those trees without something sending him off track, and I also know a large branch was found near-by that could have been used by Jet to cause Pete's head injury.' Richard took another sip of tea. 'All I know is if I had reacted a little quicker I might have been able to save my friend.'

'Don't think like that Richard. Everything must have happened so quickly that there would have been nothing you could have done.' Veronica patted his hand. 'I could never believe that Jet killed his father. I was convinced it was an accident and maybe it was, but maybe it wasn't. There is no proof either way, just what Richard thinks he saw. There was no reason for Jet to kill his father, he wasn't left any money in the will, but when the red mist comes down, I don't think he knows what

he's doing himself sometimes.

'The estate was put into trust until after my death. That

was when Jet really went off the rails. You can turn
yourself into a pretty good drug addict even on his small
allowance. Eventually I tracked him down, or rather
Jonathan Parker did, and we got him into rehab. I
thought he was over this. I really thought he had sorted
himself out and got a respectable job. Where did it all
go wrong?' Veronica started to cry and Richard held her
tight.

Jenny wasn't really sure what to do. Veronica was right,

all these things that Jet was being accused of, there was
no real hard evidence. Nothing they could go to the
police with. Maybe he had just been in the wrong place
at the wrong time. If so, who else was trying to hurt
her?

Veronica moved away from Richard and stood by the
fireplace facing Jenny.
'You are probably right about Jet. I have been blinded
by a mother's love but I don't want to do anything to
harm him.' Veronica said.

'I need to find out for definite if his is the one trying to hurt my friends and stop him. I going to resurrect the club and I won't pay for his protection.'

'So do you have a plan?' Richard said.

'What I would like to do is to bring Mike and Jet together, I'll provide the money Mike owes Jet and we will try to get Jet to admit everything to Mike. We have no real proof so we need Jet to think we have, and be frightened enough to confess.'

'Not a bad idea,' Richard smiled.

'Okay I think it sounds okay, but I need time to process everything,' Veronica said. 'And I think you need time to find Mike?' She looked over at Jenny who nodded. 'I will ring you tomorrow, once I've slept on it and we can then agree what has to be done next.'

'Sounds good,' Jenny smiled.

'And thank you for listening to us Veronica.' Richard smiled and gave her one last hug as they left.

As they left Veronica's, Richard asked Jenny if she had plans. When she said she hadn't, he drove them to Wollaton Park. It was coming up to Christmas and the hill leading up to the hall had lanterns hanging from light strings promenading the walk. The hall was lit from below making it look like it was rising from some sort of underground chamber with a mist around its base. Jenny was glad she had wrapped up warm and gone for flat boots, when Richard suggested a walk. They rounded the hall and started to walk down towards the lake. Triggered by the onset of darkness, the whole of the lake area lit up. All the trees contained strings of blue bulbs and in the lake there were floating lights of different colours swaying with the movement of the water. A white duck had fallen asleep on top of one of them and he looked like a flamingo as the red glow reflected off his pale plumage.

'I hope it's not too cold for you.' Richard clapped his hand together to try to get the circulation flowing.

'I am fine. Thanks,' Jenny said waving a sheepskin mitt covered hand at him. 'But if it will help, you can hold my hand.' She grinned.

'That would be very much appreciated, but we'll have to swap hands half way round so I get the full benefit.'

'I think we could manage that.'

'Can I ask you a question?' Richard looked down at the floor and then up at Jenny through his eyelashes.

She hadn't noticed how long his lashes were before, and how they framed his soft blue eyes.

'Jenny?' he said shaking her back into reality.

'Of course, as long as I can refuse to answer.'

171

'How does an obviously intelligent woman like you end up as a stripper?'

'Does it bother you,' she scowled

'No. Not at all, I am just intrigued to know.'

Jenny smiled to show she had only been teasing, 'Well I fell into it really. I needed some cash when I first left the home and so I got a bar job in the club. The girls in the club really took me to their hearts and once I saw how much extra they could earned with tips I couldn't see why I would want to carry on behind the bar. Plus the rules are you can't grope the strippers, but the punters think that the girls delivering drinks are fair game. So I actually get touched up less as a stripper than I did as a bar girl.'

'You said the home, does that mean you were in care?' Richard looked at her carefully.

'Hang on a minute, let's do this one question for you, one question for me.'

'Okay, ask away.'

'How come an attractive man like you, with all your money, hasn't got a wonderful wife running the social side at home? Or have you?' Jenny stopped smiling as she waited for the answer..

'I suppose you could say that I'm married to the job.'

'Come on, that hardly gives as much as I just gave.' By this time they had walked about half way around the lake so Richard quickly swapped sides and held Jenny's other hand. As she raised an eyebrow, he waved his un-gloved hand at her and they both started giggling. 'Okay, more details. My father left me and my mum when I was very small and she had to take lots of small jobs, so that we could get by. She never wanted to rely on benefits. When I finished my A levels, she insisted that I go to university and she would carry on working to help me out. I didn't want her to do that. I agreed to go to university part time and I got a job at Pharmcorp as an intern for the rest of the time. That's when I first met Charlie.

'It turned out I was a rubbish chemist but I had a feel for the product. If the chemists said a drug would do one thing, I would ask if they could do something else with it and with a few tweaks they usually could. It turns out these tweaks made the product unique and gave Pharmcorp a massive advantage in getting drugs to market before other companies had even thought of it. I graduated and Charlie persuaded me to work for him full time, but after a few years I got bored. Charlie gave me a loan to start Daniels and I finally managed to pay him back last summer. But this has all taken a lot of my time. Mum got sick a few years ago so when I wasn't at work I was looking after her. She died and I spent more time at work. I could say I've just never met the right woman but I never would, unless she had just walked into my office.' Richard spun her round and looked into her eyes. 'Just like you did.'

'Wow nicely done, you would definitely be able to charm any women who did just happen to walk into your office. But we are back at the start of the lake so it must be the end of questions and time to go home.'
'Maybe, but I have more questions so don't expect me to be vanishing any time soon.'

Chapter sixteen – Catching Jet

The next day Veronica was still thinking about the conversation she had had with Jenny and Richard, when Jet turned up.

'Hi Mom, how ya doing?' Jet kissed her on the cheek and helped himself to some toast. He sat down opposite her at the breakfast table in the conservatory. The sun was shining through the glass even though it was a bitterly cold day.

'Not too bad, thank you darling,' Veronica smiled. 'What brings me the company of my favourite son this fine morning?'

'I was just passing through and thought I would pop in and check on you. Can't a son just check in every now and then?'

'Of course. You don't usually pop in.'

'Well I did today.'

They sat in silence whilst Veronica finished her breakfast and, as she poured herself a second cup of tea, she looked up at her son.

'Well while I am here,' he smiled. 'I don't suppose you could loan me a couple of hundred pounds, just until the end of the month.'

'I knew there had to be a reason for this visit. I thought business was good.' She tried to be harsh with him but knew she would fold eventually.

'I have a small cash flow problem and I will have it sorted by the end of the month.'

'And what is this cash flow problem?'

'There's a guy who owes me some money and he'll have it by the end of the month.'

Veronica didn't want to push it any further but she thought she would try one more question. 'I can't do it this time. I have cash flow problems myself. Until Charlie's company can be sold I don't have much spare cash. It's all down to this friend of Charlie's holding up the sale. Did I tell you he left some shares to a stripper? She worked at some club called the Blue Lagoon Gentleman's Club. Would you believe it?' Veronica kept a close eye on her son and the minute she mentioned the club his faced dropped, but he recovered very quickly.

'Come on, I know you can spare a couple of hundred.'

'I'll see what I can do. I'll call you later if I can raise some. Okay?

'Sounds good.' Jet kissed his mother on the cheek and left.

After Jet left she phoned Jenny and told her she would help with the plan but she didn't want any police involved, just the threat.

Earlier that same day Jenny was woken early by a telephone call from Jonathan Parker, saying he had located Mike Peters. He gave her a contact number. Jenny then set about organising the confrontation that needed to take place the following morning.

The next morning Jenny and Richard were enjoying breakfast in Veronica's conservatory when Jet entered.

His face fell as he saw them.

'Why Richard, long time no see. How are you?' Jet strode across the conservatory and heartily shook Richard's hand. 'And I don't believe I have had the pleasure.' He smiled at Jenny and bent in a protracted bow, kissing her hand at the same time.

'This is Charlie's friend I was telling you about, Jenny,' smiled Veronica.

'Well it is a pleasure to meet you. Good Morning Mother. Is this not a good time? I thought it would be just the two of us.'

'No. This is a perfect time.' Veronica rang a small bell she had next to her on the table. 'The problem is, as I said yesterday I have a small cash flow problem of my own and so Jenny has come up with a solution to your problem,' said Veronica as the conservatory door opened and Mike walked in. Jet was brilliant at keeping his cool and looked questioningly at his mother.

'I'm sorry, but who is this?' Jet looked around the group, waiting for an explanation.

'Come on Jet, It's me, Mike. You must remember me. After all you burnt my club down only last week.'

'I don't know what's going on here but I've never seen this man before in my life.'

'I think you have Jet,' his mother scolded him. 'Jenny and some of her friends have seen you at the club so we know you're familiar with this man.'

'But you must understand the cash wasn't for me. I have a boss. I am just the collector.'

Richard stood and looked Jet in the eye. 'Then you need to tell us who your boss is Jet because Jenny's going to take over the club and when it's back up and running, she will not be paying anyone anything.'

'There's no way I'm going give up one of the hardest men in Nottingham to an aging bouncer and a stripper. Do you think I'm mad?'

'Maybe not but I'm sure the police might have a little more pull. Burning down the club and beating up Jenny

178

is going to leave you with a lengthy sentence if you don't give up your boss.'

'I don't know what you are talking about,' Jet said. He looked steadily at each one of them. 'I never touched her, or her friends.'

They all stood there staring at him, not one of them offering him any help.

'Alright there is no boss. It's just me. But you left me with no choice.' Jet glared at his mother. She held his gaze as he continued. 'I have no skills and no inheritance. What was I supposed to do?'

'It's not as if you tried anything else, is it?' Veronica yelled. 'You have contacts, Charlie, Vicki and Richard. Did you go to any of them and try to get a job?'

'Why would they help me?'

'Because they are our friends and as long as you are willing to work and don't expect to be handed everything on a plate, they will help you out.' Veronica now stood up and walked over to her son. Holding his hand, she looked him straight in the eye. 'I have convinced Jenny and Mike not to go to the police this time, but you have thirty days to find yourself a real job and prove you can make an honest living. If you can't do that, or fall back to your old ways, Jenny has friends in the police force who will track you down. Do you understand?'

Jet's eyes dropped to the floor and he nodded.

'I will try but it's so hard. It was easy to threaten Mike once I had something on him. You really should have called my bluff.' Jet smiled at Mike.

'But all the damage you've done to the club, beating up Jenny. Why do that if it was just a bluff?' Mike said.

'I said before, I don't know what you mean. I honestly never touched Jenny. I was at my narcotics anonymous meeting when she was attacked. I have a room full of people who can back me up. I was at the club this morning before the fire started but I swear I didn't start it. Why would I? You're not going to pay without a club are you?'

'Look, I think I'd like you all to leave now so I can talk to my son.' Veronica said.

As they walked out to the car Mike turned to Jenny and said, 'I don't know how to thank you for this.'

'I do. Sell me the club.' She smiled.

'But it is just a burnt out shell.'

'Well, it did need a makeover anyway.'

'If you're sure.'

'I am, and to prove it we have an appointment with Mr McGuffin to sign the papers. So if you want to sell...'

'Yes please.'

'Right let's go.'

The next few weeks were tied up with Jenny looking at designs for the club and how to make it look like a modern strip club. She put in a front bar for people who wanted to have a quiet drink and had separate rooms for men and women. Jenny felt the way forward was women watching men strip, not the other way round. She planned to advertise as the first strip club for women in Nottingham. She was also playing with the idea of having specialist nights for gay and lesbian groups. She didn't really know yet how it was all going to work, but she knew she had to be different, and she was going to try everything she could think of to give her club the edge. And the first thing was to change its name.

Wednesday morning was one of the coldest of the year and Jenny left the builders at it and headed off to the

café. She wandered into the café and headed straight to
the back to place her order.

'Milkie coffee and a bacon butty please, Silvie.' Jenny
smiled; she was getting to be a regular since the
rebuilding of the club had started.

'Coming right up. Why don't you go and join your
friend and I'll bring them over and maybe another cup
of coffee for her.' Silvie smiled and nodded towards a
booth that Jenny had walked straight past not even
noticing the occupant. She turned round to see, fast
asleep, with her head lying on the table, Vicki Swansen.

'Looks like she could do with a bacon butty too. I'll go
and check on her.'

Jenny sat opposite Vicki and gently shook her
shoulders. Vicki moved slightly muttered something
incomprehensible and continued to sleep. Jenny shook
her again, a little more forcibly and Vicki very slowly
raised her head and half opened her eyes. She looked at
Jenny and then her eyes flew open.

'Oh my god, I am so sorry. I hope they don't think I'm
some down and out coming in for a warm and a sleep.'
Vicki glanced round, smiling at the staff standing round
the counter and the cook area.

'Vicki what are you doing here?' Jenny knew Vicki had
been very uncomfortable when they had met here before

and she couldn't believe she'd suddenly taken a shine to the place.

'I was looking for you and I didn't really want to come and ask you for advice, so I thought if we bumped into each other accidentally, it wouldn't look so obvious.'

Silvie came over and placed two cups of coffee and two bacon butties between them. 'And I seem to remember the coffee was fantastic.' Silvie brought over a bottle of HP and the sugar bowl.

'You wanted to ask ME for advice? I hardly think there is anything I could help you with. Although you do look exhausted what's going on?'

'Well that's the problem. I have been working at Pharmcorp trying to prove to everyone that I can do as good a job as my father did, but I can't understand how he did it. I am trying to survive on four hours sleep a night. I am working every hour I'm awake and I still don't seem to get anything done.'

'Has Terry been helping you? And the other staff?'

'Yes. Everyone has been great but there was so much stuff Charlie just knew after forty years doing this type of thing. I have to look things up and every time I make a decision I'm checking it three or four times before I am happy. Even then I am not sure I've done the right

thing.'

'Have you thought that this is just too much for you? If I

remember you told me your degree was in literature, not

chemistry.'

'It was but I don't need to know chemistry to run the

business. I was going to do an MBA to make sure I had

the business stuff down pat but I don't know when I will

find the time.' Vicki was chocking back the tears.

'Okay let's eat our breakfast, drink our coffee, and after

that I will put my thinking cap on.'

Vicki wiped away a tear, nodded and reached for the

HP sauce.

After breakfast Jenny ordered two more coffees and sat

down opposite Vicki with her serious face on.

'Right it seems to me that you're too exhausted to make

any sensible decisions right now.' Vicki was about to

interrupt but when she saw the look of determination on

Jenny's face she changed her mind.

'You need to seriously consider whether this is what you

really want to do. It will get easier but if you don't love

it now, what's going to change?' Jenny took a sip of her

coffee and when Vicki didn't answer she carried on.

'There's an opportunity to sell the business for a lot of

money, and from what I can see, your dad was in favour

of this buy out. All the staff are financially taken care

of, even if they don't get to keep their jobs. This

opportunity won't present itself again. If the buyout

goes through you will be a very rich woman and be able

to set yourself up in business. There is even the

publishing house. I know Cecil was left it in the will,

but I am sure we could talk to him and see if there is

anything you could do there.'

Vicki looked up and slowly sipped her coffee. 'I think

you're right. I am too tired to make a decision but I don't

want to let Dad down with the business.'

'And you won't. I am sure all he wanted was for you to

be happy, not exhausted and making yourself ill to

continue his dream. You need to get your own dream

started and then you'll see.'

'I think I'll go home, have a hot bath and get some sleep.

Then I'll think about it all. Thanks for your help.'

'Don't mention it. And Vicki, next time, just give me a

call. You can always come and talk to me.'

Vicki smiled and slowly got up. 'Will do. But first I

think a hot bath and a good long sleep are called for.'

Chapter seventeen – A New Club and a decision

The club was nearing completion and Jenny hadn't seen the girls in a while so she invited them all for dinner. She had added a kitchen and the club was going to offer a basic but wholesome range of food with comical names. Hopefully getting the parties in to eat, would expand her clientele and keep them there all night. She had also put in a dance room just for a disco with dancers, like they had where Mindy was working in Derby. She had expanded the club upstairs and the changing rooms had been split into two, males and females, and heated to help keep the dancers happier and healthier, too much time was lost with dancers being off with cold or the flu.

The girls arrived together and Carly was chatting ten to the dozen as they walked through the doors. She had not seen Mindy or Blossom, since Blossom had been discharged from hospital. As they entered the club all three fell silent and stared. The entrance was light and contained a cloak room and had pine panelled floors and walls.

Jenny rushed up and gave then all a hug.

'How are you all? It's been too long. Everything has been a bit mental.' Jenny smiled. 'Carly how did the exams go, Blossom how are you felling and Mindy, I heard about you brother, tell me all about it.'

186

'Whoa hold on a minute,' Carly smiled. 'If the rest of the place is as impressive as the entrance, it looks like you've got a grand tour to give before we tell you any of our news.'

Jenny grinned madly. 'I've worked so hard, I hope you like it. Let's put your coats in the cloak room and then we can go on the tour.'

As they approached the cloakroom window, Mike popped up from behind the counter.

'Mike,' they all squealed at once. 'What are you doing here? We missed you.'

'Jenny asked me to help out whilst she gets the club up and running again. I don't know what I would have done without her.' He smiled and grabbed Jenny's hand.

'You know there will always be a job here for you.'

Jenny squeezed his hand back. 'Right, the tour.'

Jenny led them through a set of double doors into the restaurant/dance area which was well lit and had wooden floors. The walls were covered in mosaics of semi-naked men and women. They looked similar to the murals on the walls of roman baths; tasteful but still strangely erotic. Jenny nodded and, hidden from sight, Mike flicked a switch so the lights dimmed and the disco lights showed. After the girls had stopped clapping and cheering the lights came back up and

Jenny led them through a door to the left. This room was in the style of the old strip club. Red lighting and a long catwalk stage with stools along the stage and small tables scattered around the room. The bar ran the length of the room and had been fully fitted with all the latest back lights. Mike dimmed the lights and smoke started rising from the stage. The girls couldn't believe their eyes.

Jenny led them back to the restaurant and out through a door to the right. There was a flight of stairs and at the top an old fashioned conference type room which had a video screen, and a plinth for a speaker to stand behind. The final room was back down the stairs and off to the right and was identical to the room on the left of the restaurant except the colours were more pinks and purples.

As they returned to the restaurant, a table had been laid out ready for them to enjoy lunch.

'The red room is for the old school guys and the pink room is for ladies to watch male strippers,' Jenny explained.

'So want about that boring room upstairs?' Blossom asked.

'I'm thinking we might be able to use it as a conference room for local businesses.'

'Yeh right, because big business is going to want to hold conferences in a strip club,' Carly scoffed.

'Hang on.' Jenny said. 'If we have the facilities and are cheap enough they aren't going to care. There is a separate door so they don't have to go through the club and the club won't be busy during the day.'

'Well I think you're mad.' Carly continued.

'It only cost an extra couple of grand to do, as part of the refit. There's no need to hide this club up a back alley like we're ashamed of it any more. It's time everyone knew the name.'

'So with these changes are you keeping the name?' Mike asked.

'If you don't mind Mike, I thought we'd call it Charlie's' Jenny said.

'What a great idea,' Mike smiled and raised his glass.

'To Charlie's'

'To Charlie's,' they chorused and chinked their glasses.

They sat down and were served by two waiters dressed in black.

'The real opening won't be for a few weeks. I need to get the safety checks and certificates completed but I am going to start advertising and who knows I might get some Christmas parties if I'm lucky. Now then you know what I've been up to so what about you guys?' Jenny said as she took a forkful of salad.

'I've been fairly uneventful, so I'll go first,' Carly jumped in. 'I had my exams the day after Blossom was discharged and since then I have been getting ready to try and sort out my next placement. It is strange as you have to put your applications in even before you know if you have passed the exam or not.'

'Does this mean you will have to move away?' Mindy looked worried, she liked her little gang and didn't want them to split up.

'Well luckily, I passed my exam, but I can't stay at Queen's Medical Centre, I've already done one placement there. But as I did so well, I got my first choice placement and that is at...'

'Oh, come on don't keep us in suspense,' Blossom
shouted up.
'Derby. So I can commute there or, if I move there, I
can commute here.'

'That's brilliant news. We are all so proud of you and

how well you're doing.' Jenny smiled and they all raised

their glasses to toast Carly.
'Well I have just been trying to getting better,' Blossom
looked sad that the others had been up to exciting things
but she hadn't done anything.
'In a way you did do something,' Carly said. 'You
helped us solve why Mike vanished.'
'I did?'

'Yes,' Jenny replied. 'It was because you recognised Jet

that we managed to work out what was happening with

Mike and the club. The only thing is he's adamant that

he didn't burn down the club, and I think I believe him.'

'So we still might be in danger?' Mindy gripped

Blossom's hand tightly as she spoke.

'Hopefully not for much longer.' Jenny smiled. 'The

board meeting is next week and once the vote on the

sale has been cast, there will be no need for these scare tactics.'

'I wish I knew who had been doing these things,' Mike snarled. 'I'd show 'em not to mess with me and my girls.'

'Oh Mike, you are a sweetie.' Jenny patted his hand. 'Mr Parker is still looking into it and I'm sure he'll find out who's been doing these horrible things. Anyway, let's not spoil the meal, Mindy how about you?'

'Well my life has been a revelation these last few weeks,' Mindy said. 'I met my brother while I was dancing in a club in Derby and we have met up a few times since then. He has a girlfriend and is thinking of getting married. He wants me to go to the wedding, but I am sure Mum would have a heart attack if I just turned up out of the blue. He's trying to find a way to break it to her that he's met me. He says Sunil has gone back to India and gotten himself a good subservient wife. As he never divorced me, if he comes back, I can get him done for bigamy.'

192

'Well done Mindy and you are looking so much happier.'

They toasted Mindy and then spent the rest of the afternoon tasting all the items from the new menu and talking about how they all wanted to get back to the club.

The next morning, Jenny was nursing a mild hangover when the front door bell rang. She slowly rushed, as you only can do when you have a hangover, and friends staying and don't want to wake them, but every time you move your head hurts, and answered the door. Standing very erect at the door, but panicking about the fact he had left his car outside unattended, was Richard Pickles chauffeur.

'Good morning maam. I have come to collect you for the board meeting.' He was professional to the end and didn't flinch when her saw her still in her kimono dressing gown, with the hair on the left side of her head pointing straight up, from where she had slept on it.

'Board meeting?'

'Yes, for Pharmcorp.'

'That's not until next week. The twenty third.'

'It's the twenty third today.'

'You're joking. Argh.'

'Please don't panic maam. The meeting is not until eleven and it is now only nine but Mr Pickles wondered if you would like to meet him for breakfast before the meeting. He said he did try to call, but you were not answering your phone, so he was a little worried.'

Jenny scanned around and saw her phone on top of the kitchen work surface. She checked and there were five missed calls. She must have forgotten to take it off silent, after they had finished talking last night.

'That would be lovely but as you can see I am not quite ready yet. Why don't you go back to the car? I shall get ready and come down to you. I'll be about half an hour so if you need to drive round, please do.' Jenny said.

The chauffeur shoulders slumped making him look far more relaxed and he agreed to be parked outside at nine thirty.

Jenny dived through the shower and went with very neutral basic make up and brushed her hair leaving it long and straight. The next question was what did one wear for a board meeting? She most certainly did not want to show herself up, but the new clothes she had bought had been casual clothes. She always felt more at home in jeans, a good pair of boots and a nice top that she did in a suit. Leafing through her wardrobe the only thing she had that was appropriate was the suit she had worn for Charlie's funeral. Well there was no time to get anything else so she went with it. Pairing it with a new silk shirt that was cornflower blue with oriental swirls and patterns in yellows and oranges covering it. It really set off the blue in her eyes. She hoped no one would notice she only had one suit. At exactly nine thirty she was down stairs and ready as the car pulled up to collect her.

Five minutes later she was walking into a flat that was on the same floor in this block as hers was across the city, but there the similarity ended. The flat was one great big room with the kitchen and lounge as you walked in and a bed at the other end. The only thing she couldn't see was a bathroom, and she assumed, that was through the only door the room had to offer. The floors were covered in a carpet that you sunk into as you walked across it, and the walls had murals painted onto the plain brick. There was a huge window on each of the side walls and the way the morning light fell on the bed there had to be a skylight over it. Richard was sat at the table in the kitchen area reading the financial times. As she walked in he rushed over and gave her a hug, she winced ever so slightly.

'What is it? Have you been hurt?' Richard asked, he looked her up and down.

'No, no. It's just the ibuprofen hasn't quite kicked in yet. Once I've had something to eat I'll be fine.' Jenny said and smiled at him. She was really glad he had been worried. It meant he cared.

'Oh, I see. I was so worried about you after everything that has happened.'

'But you know we sorted Jet out, so everything is okay again, isn't it?' She looked at him as if to say, he wasn't to worry.

'Yes, but he says he didn't start the fire or attack you. I'm not sure I believe him but if he's telling the truth, there's still someone out there determined to hurt you.'

'And once today's meeting is over there'll be no need for anyone to try and frighten me off will there?'

'I suppose not but I'd still rather we'd caught the bastard. In future can you at least answer your phone to let me know you're okay?'

'Yeh, sorry about that but I was having a get together with the girls and after we finished at the club, we all went back to mine and just chatted and drank until the early hours. They are all still there now.'

'Shall we have some breakfast and then we can talk about the board meeting if you like.'

They sat down at the breakfast table and Jenny couldn't believe her eyes. The table was covered with a selection of fruits, breads, croissants, cheeses and some cooked meat.

'Wow, did you think I would be hungry?' Jenny joked.

'I wasn't sure what you liked for breakfast so I chose everything.'

'Usually I have a bacon butty and a coffee but I think with this hangover the fresh fruit might be a good starting point. I would still love a coffee.'

'Of course,' Richard got up and walked over to the breakfast counter where there was a coffee machine identical to the one in his office. The man obviously appreciated a good cup of coffee.

After breakfast they settled down to talk about the board meeting.

'I can't believe I forgot the meeting was today.' Jenny said, she was normally so conscientious about remembering dates.

'Things have been a little unusual and frantic for you recently, haven't they?'

'To tell you the truth I was so excited about the club I forgot all about Pharmcorp. The fact I am a shareholder and need to help make this decision still seems so weird.'

'And have you made your decision?'

'Yes. I am happy that I have made the right choice, but it depends how the others vote. I think with my vote Terry St John should have enough votes, but I don't really want to alienate Vicki and Veronica, I feel like we have become friends over the last few months. I had a chat with Vicki last week and I hope she's thought through her options. She was so exhausted and so unhappy, trying to continue her father's dream. I told her "That was his dream and she needed to follow her own dream," but I don't know if she will have listened to me or not.'

'Sounds to me like you know what you are doing. Shall we get you to that meeting?'

'Yes please.'

Chapter eighteen – Decision made

The Board Meeting was held in the Pharmcorp offices in the centre of Nottingham and Jenny was the first to arrive at the board room. Vicki and Terry were in their respective offices still working. Veronica arrived a few minutes after Jenny and they chatted for a while about how well Jet was doing. He had gone back into rehab and Veronica was hoping if he could get an honest job, working with good people, he might finally turn a corner.

At exactly eleven o clock, Terry and Vicki and a number of people Jenny didn't recognise entered the room and the meeting started. The first thirty minutes were the formalities of a board meeting with the reading of previous minutes and talking over a few points that had arisen. Then it was time for the vote. Terry, as the acting chairman, read out the offer and asked everyone to confirm they understood and were happy to vote on it.

Everyone nodded and Vicki asked Terry if it would be possible for her to have the floor. Terry looked nervous, he knew she didn't want the buy out to go ahead, and he thought he had just enough votes for the motion to carry. He didn't want Vicki to change even one person's mind as it could jeopardise the whole deal. However he couldn't really refuse so he sat and allowed Vicki to speak.

'I know many of you are aware I am not in favour of this deal.' Vicki started and then looked around the room. She took a drink of water and continued. 'This company was my father's dream and he, with the help of Terry St John and some of you, built it up from nothing to a company that today is in a position to consider a three billion pound buy out. I felt that the best way to continue his work, was to continue the company, in the way he did and I have spent the last two months working with you, trying to understand the best direction for the business. I have taken advice from people who know the business,' she looked over a nodded at Terry.

'And people who knew my father,' she looked over at Jenny and her mother, 'and I have come to the conclusion that I am not my father. Whilst I would have given my all for this company and tried my best to help it to grow and prosper, a buy out of this magnitude is a once in a lifetime opportunity. All the staff will be provided for and I have spoken to Bensons and they have assured me that anyone who wants a job with them will be kept on.' She took another sip of water, licked her lips and continued.

'I think my father was very proud of this business.

Looking at the contract and the person who he brought in to talk sense into us all,' again she looked at Jenny, 'I think he would have wanted this deal to go through. And therefore I am recommending to the board and all the shareholders that we agree this buy out, and enjoy the rewards my father worked so hard to achieve.' The whole room burst into a round of applause and both Terry and Veronica sat staring at Vicki.

The vote was then held and it was unanimous, Bensons were going to buy Pharmcorp and the people sat around the table were about to become very rich.

Terry pushed an intercom buzzer and two minutes later one of the secretaries arrived with champagne. Terry opened the bottles and poured.

'To a great deal.' Terry said and raised his glass to the assembled group and then turned and raised his glass to Vicki, thanked her, turned and raised his glass to Jenny and silently mouthed thank you to her. Whilst everyone was toasting and discussing the deal Vicki walked over to Jenny.

'Thanks for your advice about this.' Vicki smiled. 'I think I knew all along but I just needed someone to spell it out for me.'

'Well as long as you don't think I forced you into it,' Jenny said.

'No not at all. I just need to figure out what I am going to do next.'

'Weren't you interested in publishing?'

'Oh yes, I would love to do something in publishing. But what if I'm no good at that as well?'

'Are you willing to start at the bottom?'

'That's probably a good idea. I don't need the money anymore, so perhaps starting at the bottom will check whether I enjoy it and teach me the proper way to do something. Why, do you have an idea?'

'My friends Mindy and Blossom are meeting with Cecil Moreau tomorrow, to talk over the book he is commissioning about their lives. Why don't you come with us and we can see if there is anything you can do.'

'That would be brilliant. Let me see if I can find anything in Dad's papers about the publishing house and I will read up on it tonight.'

'Great, I'll pick you up on the way in tomorrow,' as Jenny and Vicki were finishing their conversation, Richard Pickles appeared outside the board room window and waved.

'Looks like you're wanted,' Vicki smiled and winked

'Stop it.' Jenny blushed, grabbed her bag and headed out of the room. 'See you tomorrow.'

'How did it go?' Richard asked as she came out of the room.

'Good. Unanimously in favour.'

'Wow, how did that happen? I thought Vicki was dead against it.'

'We had a chat a few days ago. I think she realised she could do more harm than good if she wasn't careful. She wasn't confident she could grow the business so she needed to agree to the deal. Tomorrow I'm helping her find a new job; something she'll enjoy.'

'Jenny Cartwright you never cease to amaze me.' Richard shook his head and smiled. 'Now are you free for the rest of the day?'

'Apart from three hung-over women probably still lounging around in my flat and builders who are perfectly capable of finishing off the club by themselves, I don't believe I have anything else that requires my attention.'

'Excellent. Then let's go do something. I have a surprise for you.'

As they came out of the offices the car was waiting for them and Richard opened the door so Jenny could slide in. He slid in the other side and as the chauffeur began to pull away Richard poured them both a glass of champagne.

'This is my second glass today and that's on top of what's still in my system from yesterday and a couple of ibuprofen. Are you trying to take advantage of me?'

'Let me promise you, when I do try to take advantage of you I want you to be fully compus mentus.'

They drove for about twenty minutes and then pulled onto a large empty field. As they headed over the bough of a small hill, parked on a small square of cement Jenny saw a helicopter. Jenny looked over at Richard. He smiled and nodded.

They got into the helicopter and Jenny realised Richard was going to be flying. They set off. At first she was clinging on to her seat, not knowing what to think or do, but once they had been in the air a few minutes she started to relax. Richard was obviously an accomplished pilot and the view was so amazing, she forgot to be frightened, and started to enjoy herself. They flew low and Jenny was amazed by how much she could see, and how effortlessly they seemed to move through the sky. In what seemed like no time at all they were coming down to land. They landed on the lawn of what looked like a stately home and Richard whisked her inside. They shared a lunch and then spent the afternoon being pampered in the spa. After a fantastic afternoon Richard asked her if she would like to stay for dinner and Jenny agreed. The meal was nearly as good as the food she had had at Raymond Blanc's restaurant.

'I can't believe all these wonderful places you take me to,' Jenny said to Richard as they were enjoying a glass of brandy.

'I can't believe you keep agreeing to come with me. You are an amazing, intelligent woman and I really enjoy your company. I know you haven't told me much about yourself but I think you haven't had the best of starts in life. Everyone that meets you asks your advice and so far, from what I've seen, it's always sensible and well thought through. I think you deserve everything life can give you.'

'Well that is very nice of you, but I think you may have overestimated me.'

'I don't think so,' Richard smiled. 'We need to get going if I'm going to fly you back tonight.'

'I don't suppose there would be any way we could leave the flight back until tomorrow?' Jenny smiled.

Chapter nineteen – New beginnings

The next morning while Jenny and Richard were still snuggled up together somewhere miles from Nottingham, Vicki was trying to get hold of her. She had tried her mobile numerous times and then given up and decided to try her land line.

'Hello,' Mindy said as she picked up Jenny's phone.

'Oh thank god, is Jenny there?' Vicki said sounding more panicked than she needed to be.

'No, we haven't seen her since yesterday morning. Who is this?'

'It's Vicki Swansen here and I need to get hold of Jenny,'

'Well this is Mindy and I had assumed she was still with you. Didn't she go to some meeting with you yesterday morning?'

'Yes she did but that was finished by lunch time. She left with Richard Pickles. She must still be with him.'

'Nice,' Mindy said. 'Well as it looks like Jenny is tied up, not literally I hope, can I help?'

'Maybe you can. Jenny had suggested I could go and talk to Cecil Moreau and see if there were any jobs going at the publishing house and she said you were going to see him today.'

'That's right we need to go and meet a ghost or something.'

'Do you think I can tag along? Maybe you could introduce me to Cecil.'

'Yeh, why not. We're still at Jenny's flat at the moment.

When we woke up yesterday we were a little hung-over, and Jenny has better DVD's than me so we decided to hang out here. The problem is we need to get back over to Hyson Green, to my flat, to get changed before the meeting and then back to Castle Boulevard all by eleven and you know what buses are like.'

'I'm ready now so why don't I collect you from Jenny's and then we can use my car to get you about town a little quicker.'

'That would be brilliant. When can you be here?'

'Give me ten minutes and then meet me outside.'

Vicki pulled up outside the flats and parked on double yellow lines waiting for Mindy and Blossom. She was in deep discussion with a traffic warden as the girls exited the building.

'Give us a break Perky,' Blossom called, as she saw who was talking to Vicki.

'Oh hey Blossom. Sorry didn't realise it was you,' he looked at Vicki. 'You should have said you were waiting for Blossom.'

Blossom gave him a peck on the cheek and got into the back of the car.

'Club reopens in a few weeks, I see if I can get you an invite.' Blossom called.

'Sweet,'

'Let's get going before someone we don't know tries to give you a ticket,' Blossom called from the back seat.

'He's one of the regulars at the club. Because traffic wardens, policemen, bin men all work strange hours they tend to come to the club in the afternoon, you get to know them. It never hurts to be friendly with these guys,' Mindy smiled. 'I'm Mindy, that's Blossom and I am hoping you're Vicki, or we're in the wrong car.'

'Yes I'm Vicki and I must say you two are nothing like I expected.'

'We don't wear our stripper gear all the time you know.' Blossom sulked from the back seat.

'No it's just I thought all strippers had to look like Jenny.'

'They do in most clubs. That why our club is special. A bit of variety makes the world go around don't you think?'

'Definitely. Mindy, do you want to give me some directions?'

After a frantic rush across Nottingham, through the one way system, dodging trams along the way, they arrived at VVC publishing house at exactly eleven. As they parked Mindy rushed out of the car and flung her arms around a tall good looking Asian man standing just outside the entrance.

'Wow. Is that her boyfriend?' Vicki asked Blossom.

'I assume it must be her long lost brother. They met by accident a few weeks ago and they've been building bridges ever since. It looks like he's going to help fill in some bits in Mindy's story. What happened at home after they threw her out and what happened to her bastard of a husband.'

'So you guys have had it tough?'

'Sure have. Without Jenny and Mike, I would be dead by now. I'm not sure about Mindy but she definitely wouldn't be the happy girl she is today.'

'Jenny's a really great lady isn't she?'

'She sure is and I hope this all works out for her. I was worried when she said she was going to offer Jet a job but he's turned out great. He has really helped with the rebuild and she's now looking to get him a job when the club opens.'

'What. Jenny has offered Jet a job? After everything

he's done to you guys?'

'Jenny thinks he's telling the truth about not starting the

fire.'

'But if Jet didn't do it who did?'

'Nobody knows. We're hoping now the board meeting is

over, Jenny will be safe.'

'Let's hope so. But I still can't believe she's offered Jet a

job.'

'Jenny believes in second chances and Jet needs a

break'.

'Don't you think working in a club will leave him open
to go back to drugs?'

'There will never be any drugs in our club. Too many of
us have been affected. We all look out for each other
now, and we can make sure the place stays clean. Mike
may not have been able to make the old club pay but he
kept it clean and he's still involved.'

'Well Mindy's waving, we best get inside and have a
look at what Cecil Moreau has got planned for you

guys, and I need to start begging for my first ever real job.'

The four of them entered the building and were greeted in a much friendlier manner that the first time they had visited. Coffees were fetched and all four were shown into Cecil's office and asked to wait.

'Good morning everyone. How are we all?' Cecil said as he theatrically entered the room. 'Some new faces this time?'

'Good morning Cecil,' smiled Mindy. 'This is my brother, Dilip. He's going to add a few extra bits to the story from the family's point of view, and I assume you have met Vicki Swansen, before.'

'Dilip, pleased to meet you,' Cecil shook Dilip's hand and then turned to Vicki, took her hand and kissed it. 'And I think we have only met once or twice before.'

'Yes I was wondering if we could have a chat about the publishing house?'

'Of course. Let me get these ladies and gentleman sat down with their ghost writers and then I will be back to talk to you some more. If that's okay?'

'Sure.' Vicki smiled and Cecil led the others out of the room.

After Vicki had been waiting for ages, she decided to have a little wandered round. She was sure Cecil wouldn't object. As she was getting up she noticed a manuscript on his desk entitled Treasures of Nottingham. She sat back down and started flicking through it. It appeared to be a book claiming that crusaders had travel through Nottingham and had left some treasure there that was still hidden. Vicki was just starting to enjoy the book when Cecil returned.

'Oh my dear you don't want to read that crap,' he said grabbing it from her. 'It is only on my desk so I remember to write the rejection letter. Now what was it you wanted to talk to me about?' Cecil popped the manuscript into his top draw and then wandered round the desk to settle down in the chair next to Vicki.

'Dad left me shares in Pharmcorp and now the buyout

has been approved I need to find something to do with my time. I did my degree in English Literature and I always wanted to do something in that field but with Pharmcorp and wanting to be with dad, I kind of lost my way a little. Now I am more than financially secure but I would like to see if I can follow my original dream. I was speaking to Jenny and she said you might be able to help.' Vicki smiled.

'My dear,' he smiled. 'This was your father's firm but we built it up together and he left it to me. You didn't show the slightest interest in it when he was alive and now you have nothing better to do I can see you want to push me out, try and run it yourself and then leave it in ruins once you grow bored.'

'I can assure you I want nothing of the sort. I want to learn from the bottom up and I am a little long in the tooth to go to a publishing house that doesn't know me and try to start there. I thought we could do each other a favour. I do have a considerable amount of money I could invest.'

'There you go again. Can I start at the bottom? But then you want to invest and want a say at the top. I think it would be best if you just left now.'

Vicki couldn't believe her ears and tried to argue her case but Cecil grabbed her arm and pushed her from his office. As soon as he got her to reception he turned without looking at her, and stormed back to his office. Vicki still in some state of shock turned to the receptionist and asked her to let the others know that she would be in the pub on the corner, when they were ready to leave.

Chapter twenty – David and the Templars

Vicki was sitting at the bar, debating ordering her second glass of wine, when he walked in. Six foot seven, scruffy shortest blondish hair, lean and athletic looking and dressed in khaki trousers, a brown leather jacket and a brown fedora. Just like Harrison Ford in the first Indiana Jones film, when he was still cool. He ordered a large brandy, swallowed it in one and ordered a second.

'Bad day?' Vicki asked.

'You would not believe,' he smiled and revealed perfect white teeth and wonderful corn flower blue eyes.

'Do you want to try me?'

'Well if you let me buy you another drink, I won't feel so bad about boring you with my day,' he said nodding at her empty glass.

'Well thanks to Cecil Moreau I've got nothing to do for a couple of hours so I'll have another sauvignon blanc and then you can bore away.'

He ordered the drink and they wandered over to an empty table.

'Did you say Cecil Moreau earlier?' He asked.

'Sure did. The arsehole just threw me out of his office, so I've got to sit in here until my friends have finished their business. I'm Vicki by the way.' She said as she offered her hand.

'David, David Jenkins.' He smiled and shook her hand. 'Strangely enough Cecil Moreau is the reason for my bad mood as well. Tell me your story first.'

'Nothing much to tell really. My father just died and he left the publishing house to Cecil.'

'Your father was Charlie Swansen?'

'Sure was,' she nodded and continued. 'Well I studied English Literature at university and I thought now that I am jobless, long story, I would like to get into publishing. So a friend of mine suggested I go and ask Cecil if there were any jobs going. While my friends were there he was lovely but when we were alone he got all aggressive. He accused me of trying to push him out and take over and then he threw me out.'

'Wow what an arse.' David whistled through his teeth.

'I know. So as you can see I am not his biggest fan.'

'Well my story is a little longer than yours was, so would you let me buy you some lunch? The food here is great, good old fashioned pub grub.'

'That would be lovely thank you,' Vicki smiled.

Vicki was flicking through a magazine that had been left on the table while David was at the bar.

'Hello there. Today's your lucky day,' Vicki looked up to see Marissa tottering over towards David.

'I think it might be,' David smiled and glanced over

towards Vicki. 'How can I help you?'

'I popped in for a drink, but I hate to drink alone, so you

get to keep me company.'

'Unfortunately it's not your lucky day. I already have

company.' David pointed towards Vicki and Marissa

turned. Vicki smiled and gave her a little wave.

'You!' Marissa spun on her five inch heels. 'You've

made one big mistake mister,' she called over her

shoulder as she stormed out.

'What was all that about?' Vicki asked David as he

returned to the table.

'No idea. I've never seen her before.'

'Really?'

'She's not my type but that figure in that dress. I think I

would remember.'

'She's my step mother.'

'No way.'

'Way. I haven't seen her since the day of my father's funeral and I have no idea why she'd be over this side of town, but she didn't seem happy to see me.' Vicki took a sip of her wine. 'Anyway enough about Marissa what about you?'

'I grew up mainly in Jerusalem where my father was in the diplomatic core and so my education was based around private tuition. I soon got ahead of where I should have been for my age. My tutor was having an affair with one of the embassy wives. If I got my work done early, he would let me go off, as long as I never told anyone. We got into the habit of having all my work done by lunch and then the afternoon was my own. There were no other boys my own age to play with so I used to go off and explore. The history of the region is fascinating and I spent more and more time exploring. I got my teacher to include the history in our lessons and when I was old enough I left and came to Nottingham University to study history and archaeology. I was fascinated by the crusaders and I loved the fact that I had chosen a city that had a link to them with the old pub.'

'I always thought the fact that the crusaders stopped at the "Trip to Jerusalem" on the way to the crusades was an urban myth.' Vicki giggled.

'So did I but I still liked the connection. Once I had completed my degree I went off for a couple of years and got a job in a museum in London but I never really settled until I decided to do some more research. I returned to Jerusalem and followed the trail of one particular band that I believe stole the Suluman's gold and escaped with it. I have traced them across Asia, through Rhodes onto Malta, through Europe and finally ended up in England and back in Nottingham. I have not found the gold but I believe I know where it is.'

David paused as the waitress walked over carrying two large plates. She place one in front of each of them and Vicki sucked in a breath when she saw the size of the fish and chips she had been served.

'So if you know where the gold is what are you waiting for?'

'I've run out of money. Funding for research looking into lost crusader's gold is very hard to come by. So I decided to write a book and I took it to Charlie. He loved it, he said even if it weren't true, people always loved a good treasure hunt book, and he would be able to sell it and help me raise some money.'

'Wow sounds great. So why has Cecil pissed you off so much?'

'Everything was going great until Charlie died. I know everything was confused and things probably got a bit mixed up but when I heard that Cecil had taken over I gave him a call to see what was happening with my book. At first he didn't return my calls, and then finally he said it was a no goer and that he would return the manuscript. When the manuscript didn't turn up after three weeks I went to his office to get it back. He told me it wasn't his fault if Royal Mail had lost it and that I should have kept a copy. I had spent months on that manuscript and I know I was stupid but I gave the memory stick to Charlie and I didn't keep another copy. So now I have no manuscript and no money for my research.'

'Wait a minute,' Vicki said. 'You know I told you Cecil threw me out of his office. He came back and found me reading a manuscript I had found on his desk.'

'And?'

'And that manuscript was all about crusader's treasure buried somewhere in Nottingham.'

'He's got it. The bastard, wait until I get my hands on him,' David jumped to his feet and started to leave the pub.

'Wait,' Vicki grabbed his arm. 'Sit down a minute and think about this. There is something weird going on. Let's finish our food and have a think about what we know.'

Vicki finished her food and pushed the plate away. 'I think we can agree there's something weird going on here. My dad would never have believed in lost crusader gold but he must have believed your book was good enough to be published. I have always wondered why dad left the publishing house to Cecil when he knew how much I loved literature but with the buyout of Pharmcorp I have been too tied up to think about it. Cecil worked with Dad on building up the business, but when all said and done he was just an employee. I think we need to delve a little deeper into Cecil Moreau and his motives and I know exactly the right people to help us. And here are some of them now.' Vicki smiled and waved as Mindy, Blossom and Dilip walked into the pub.

As everyone sat together at the pub Vicki explained what had happened.

'I don't know, they've been very good to us,' said Dilip.

'Yes they have. Treated us really nice and they didn't have to.' Blossom said and Mindy nodded.

'But that's the point,' David suddenly spoke up. 'I don't really thing they know what they are doing. As Vicki said earlier even if my story isn't true, Charlie could see it was a really good story and that it would have sold. Mainly as a boys own adventure book, but it would have sold. I don't mean to be rude but I don't see many stories out there about strippers turned good.'

Blossom started to get up. Mindy put her hand on Blossom's arm. 'He's right Blossom. I think our stories are worth telling and maybe there is a market out there, a small publishing house like VVC is hardly going to spend its money on something that isn't a certainty. And think what he's done so far, he's just spoken to us and given us four hours of a ghost writers' time.'

'But if it's no good why is he wasting his time with us?' Blossom was starting to get angry and was very confused.

'I don't know but I think we need to find out,' Vicki looked at them all. 'You said the treasure was somewhere near the Trip to Jerusalem?'

David nodded, 'That was as far as I could get with my investigation but it might be worthwhile checking out the pub and talking to the landlord to see if he knows anything about the history of the place.'

'Excellent,' Vicki smiled. 'And Dilip I need you to go back and sweet talk Cecil's secretary.'

'Me, why?' Dilip asked.

'Because she obviously took a shine to you and you are not one of us. If Cecil sees us back there he may suspect something.'

'Okay what do you want me to do?'

'Go back and chat with the secretary, pretend you want to set up another meeting for Mindy and Blossom with the ghost writer guys. See if you can find out about Cecil's movements. Anything that might help us to work out what he's up to. Then after that I'll drive us all up to the Trip to Jerusalem and we can see what we can find out there.'

Chapter twenty one – The Trip to Jerusalem

Dilip walked back to the VVC offices shaking he head. He was not sure about what they were planning to do and he was sure the wine Vicki had consumed, and the rugged and attractive man sat next to her, had turned her into some sort of conspiracy theorist. As he entered the offices the receptionist face lit up and she beamed at him. Looked like Vicki was right, he did have a fan.

'Hello there again.' he smiled.

'Hello. I didn't expect to see you again so soon.'

'Well the girls forgot to book their next appointment so they've sent me back to check when it needs to be.'

'No problems.' She thumbed through a collection of books on her desk, reading out the names on the front as she went. Included in the pile was one for Blossom's ghost writer but not Mindy's. 'Grant has taken his diary back. Can you wait whilst I go and fetch it?'

'Of course.'

As the door to the main offices closed behind her, he quickly grabbed the diary she had said belong to Cecil and started leafing through it. The most interesting thing was that he had had a couple of meetings with someone called Ben Johnson and next to his name had been marked The Trip to Jerusalem. From tomorrow Cecil was on holiday.

223

'Suzy can you call the caterers and sort out some lunch

for tomorrow's meeting,' Dilip looked up to see the door

open.

'I did it yesterday Kirk,' Suzy called back. She turned

and headed through the door just as Dilip dropped the

diary back on the top of the pile, praying that Suzy

didn't notice it was out of order.

'Sorry about that,' Suzy smiled dropping Grant's diary

on top of the pile. 'Now let's get these appointments

sorted out.

Dilip got back to the pub to find he had been nominated

the designated driver and they were heading off to The

Trip to Jerusalem. They parked the car just down the

side of the Maid Marion Way and Vicki had to admit

she was a little ashamed that they had driven what was

less than a half mile walk but they were here now.

They walked up to the front door. David was chatting to

Vicki who was behind him. He pushed the door without

looking and came to sudden stop. Before they knew it

Vicki was in his arms staring up at those cornflower

blue eyes. They both blushed and David slowly pushed

her upright and turned to face the door. He tried the

door again. It was locked. Blossom went round to try the side door through the beer garden.

'This is not one of those old fashioned pubs that closes in the afternoon is it?' David looked surprised. 'After all it is three thirty.'

'No I am sure I have drunk here in the afternoon before.' Dilip spoke up.

'Look here, the opening times are on the window and it should definitely be open,' Vicki chipped in.

'And has anyone else noticed the name of the licensee?' asked Mindy from behind them all. They all looked up at the sign over the door "Ben Johnson licensed to sell wines and spirits on these premises."

Blossom appeared from round the side of the pub followed by a small woman. She was carrying a bucket full of polish and detergents and must have been the cleaner.

'Hi everyone this is Maria. I think we should listen to what she has to say. But it's a bit cold here so let's go get a coffee and then she can fill us in on the details.'

As they all sat down and surrounded Maria, she glanced from each face and then looked down at her coffee cup. 'It is okay Maria, no need to feel nervous, just tell us why the pub is closed.' Blossom smiled and patted Maria's arm gently. Blossom was wearing her favourite electric blue shoulder length wig and very high heels. She looked anything but comforting, but Maria seemed to have taken a shine to her.

'The boss, he woke up in the night with the stomach ache. Lady boss said he was screaming from the pain and had to be rushed to the hospital. He's gonna be okay but not so good now. No time to get cover so pub closed just one night.'

'And do they know why he's ill?' Vicki asked.

'No but he had dinner with a strange man yesterday and then today he was ill. I no like the strange man he was all smiley then the boss said no and he got all angry.'

'And this was yesterday?'

'No this was three days ago. Yesterday he came back and said he was sorry and asked to buy the boss lunch. The boss said okay but the answer was still no.'

'Thanks Maria, do you know where boss man is?'

'Big hospital on the hill.'

'Queen's Medical Centre.'

'Yes that's the place.'

'I wonder what Cecil is up to?' Vicki mused to the rest of the group.

'I don't know,' said David, 'but it sound like we need to talk to the landlord and find out if he knows anymore.' David was getting as intrigued by this mystery as Vicki was. 'The problem is how do we find him and how do we know he'll talk to us.'

'Well if I'm not mistaken,' chimed in Mindy. 'Carly should be on her last week at Queen's Medical Centre this week and with any luck she can track him down. Once we know where he is, we will have to do our best to convince him to talk to us.'

Mindy rang Carly and explained what they needed. They decided to all split up, go home and get changed into some more appropriate clothes, mainly Blossom, and meet back at Holly's cafe in one hour when hopefully Mindy would have heard from Carly.

Carly managed to track Ben Johnson down quite easily, once she realised he had been brought in for a gastric intestinal illness. She didn't really want to just have the girls to go piling into his ward so she thought she would have a quick word with him herself first. As soon as she mentioned Cecil Moreau's name Ben said he would be happy to talk to the girls but the matron on duty had said no more than two visitors and Ben's wife was not leaving his side. Carly rang Mindy and it was decided to send David in to talk to Ben and his wife.

'Thank you so much for talking to me,' David smiled and shook hands with both of them. Ben Johnson

227

looked like a typical publican, overweight and jolly looking with a decent collection of tattoos except, when David met him, he had this strange greyness about him. His wife was called Hannah and was old school rock chick, long blonde hair, leather trousers and slightly more weight than she would have carried at eighteen but not so much that you would call her overweight.

'No problems.' Ben sounded positive but exhausted.

'Once we heard you had a problem with Cecil Moreau, we knew we could help you. I think he's the reason I am in here.'

'Well I won't keep you long as you are obviously tired and weaken by your illness but let me tell you why I am interested in Cecil.' David went over the details of his book and how Cecil had told him he was abandoning the project.

'Sound fishy to me.' Ben nodded. 'Cecil first came to me a few weeks ago to see if he could hire the pub for a private function. I have a very small upstairs room that I sometimes hire out but the tourist come to see the famous pub so I don't like to let them down. I would never hire out the whole pub. Cecil asked if he could hire the whole pub and said that he would bring in all his own staff and that me and Hannah could take the night off. Well I'm very proud of my pub and don't like leaving it in the hands of strangers so I said no.' Ben looked over at his wife and she poured him a glass of water. He took a long drink and leant back into his pillows, taking a deep breath. After a few minutes he opened his eyes and continued.

'Cecil turns up again three, maybe four days ago and

offers me ten thousand pounds for him to take over the whole pub for the weekend, wanted to do a murder mystery apparently and again he didn't want me or Hannah there. This time I lost me temper with him and threw him out. So then when he turns up yesterday, I was ready to throw him out again but this time he is all sweetness and light and says, he has found somewhere else to hold his party, and was sorry for going over the top. Asks if he can by me lunch. So we are eating lunch and half way through I get called away to the phone, only when I get there the phone is dead. I go back to the table and starts eating again but this time the food tastes funny. Well it's come out of me kitchen, so I don't say nothing but it didn't taste that way before I left to take the phone call. I am sure he poisoned me. The spiteful bastard.'

'And I think I might know why,' David looked serious. 'My book shows that there is a possibility that the gold is buried under the Trip to Jerusalem. I think he has poisoned you to get you out of the way so he can break in tonight, and get the treasure whilst you're in here.'

'But Hannah will be at home tonight.' Ben looked shocked and worried.

'Well I think she needs to stay with you. Do you know anyone who could help me catch him in the act?'

'I sure do. Pass me that phone and I'll get some of the boys to meet you at the pub. Do you have a plan?'

'Well if we hide out in the pub and wait until he's broken in then we can catch him at it. If he doesn't come tonight that I am sorry I have worried you unnecessarily but he will know you won't be in here for long so he will have to strike quickly.'

'Okay, and if he is there you make sure you don't stop my boys giving him the kicking he deserves.'

'Don't you think prison would be a better punishment for Cecil. Can you imagine him coping in there?'

'So true.' Ben Johnson laughed and picked up the phone ready to call some of the members of his chapter to help David catch Cecil.

Chapter twenty two – The truth will out

When David got back and told everyone about his conversation they all wanted to join him for the night of adventure. He was adamant that that was not going to happen and that with him and the hells angels boys it would be too dangerous to take anyone else with him. Vicki was not taking no for an answer. She knew there was something weird about Cecil and she didn't understand why her dad had left him the publishing house. Maybe under the pressure he would give something away.

Not knowing what time Cecil might turn up David had arranged to meet Ben Johnson's friends outside the pub at soon as they could get there. He hoped Cecil wouldn't try to do anything early in the evening, when there might be people about. They all settled down in the back bar to wait. David finally managed to get Vicki to wait up stairs, where it would be safer, but she was not happy about it. Ben's Friends were call Baz and Trev and had the physique that should scare off Cecil, when he saw them. David was hoping Cecil was too greedy to involve anyone else in the search for the gold.

Just after midnight they heard some scrapping around the side door of the pub. It was hidden from the road and the most obvious place for Cecil to enter. David, Baz and Trev silently moved into the shadows to make sure Cecil didn't see them.

'Come on, I thought you were a genius lock picker,' Cecil whispered.

'It's not a simple as it looks in the movies you know,' came back the response. David could have sworn it sounded like a woman's voice.

A few seconds later the door very slowly opened and two shadowy figures with a pen light torch entered. David put his arm out to stop Baz and Trev piling in. He wanted to make sure that they caught Cecil in the act. The two burglars made their way over to the bar and vanished behind it. There was the sound of creaking hinges and then the noise of two different foot falls going down the ladder into the cellar.

David crept to the top of the ladder so he could hear what was going on.

'Right,' whispered Cecil. 'The book says the gold will have been buried in a hidey hole in the castle walls. The castle walls are behind this wall here.'

'But that wall's twenty feet long how do we know where to look?' whisper back his assistant.

'I thought of that. I have borrowed an X-ray machine that will show up any holes behind this wall.'

For about thirty minutes there was absolute silence.

Then suddenly, 'Here, there's a gap in the rock face behind this piece of wall,' called Cecil.

'Start knocking through then,' chuckled his companion. The sound of a pick axe knocking into the wall could be heard and after ten minutes, a cheer, as Cecil found a hole behind the cellar wall.

David crept down the cellar steps followed by Baz and Trev, who were both surprisingly light on their feet for such big guys. Cecil had his head in a hole in the wall that was about three feet off the ground and his helper was standing behind him. She turned round just in time to see Trev coming do the steps.

'What the....' she shouted just as Baz grabbed hold of her and put his hand over her mouth,

'What's that Marissa?' Cecil called. When there was no response he pulled his head out of the hole and turned round to see Baz holding Marisa and David and Trev standing there.

'What the hell's going on?' Cecil demanded. 'Let go of my friend now.'

'I don't think you're in any position to demand anything

after what you've done to my mate's wall.' Baz said

looking between Cecil and the hole.

'I think, if you talk to Mr Johnson, he will confirm he

gave me permission to use his cellars tonight.'

'We've already spoken to Mr Johnson so don't come it

with us.' David said. 'Now I think it's time you

explained to us what you are doing down here.'

'You! How did you know I would be down here?' Cecil

finally recognised David and realised the game was up.

'I met a young lady this afternoon and she told me you

still had the manuscript. I always thought it was funny

that Charlie was so up for publishing the book and then

suddenly you weren't interested. When I found out this

afternoon you had been trying to get sole access to the

pub and couldn't, it all sounded a bit too fishy. Mr

Johnson is pretty pissed off and he has told these two

gentlemen here to give you a good kicking, to make up

for the pain you have put him through. It's only me

that's stopping that from happening right now.'

'Don't you understand?' Cecil looked incredulous. 'I

have found the hole. The treasure is just behind this

wall. I can see a passageway and the treasure's behind

that bend just a few hundred meters away. Don't you

understand, the five of us could finish this hole and go

234

and collect the treasure. I am sure there will be plenty enough to give Mr Johnson some to repair his wall.'

'So all along you believed the manuscript and you planned to get the gold for yourself?'

'I did I admit it. Marisa and I were going to collect the gold and make off for a life in the sun. You see she is recently widowed and hasn't been left anything so she turned to me for help and we decided to go for the gold. I realise I should have talked to you sooner but I wasn't sure how you would react. I thought you might want the treasure to go to some museum but now I see, we can work together.' Cecil was starting to sweat.

'Marissa!' Vicki had slowly come down the cellar steps whilst all this was going on. 'What the hell are you doing here?'

Baz moved his hand from over Marisa's mouth. 'What do you think I am doing here,' she spat. 'I spent all that time with your father and what did he leave me? Bog all. Do you know how painful it was, listening to him telling me all about how hard he worked and how wonderful you were? And then all I got was a couple of thousand a month and I can live in the horrible house until I die. I'm twenty two years old; I can't stay shut in the middle of nowhere for the rest of my life.'

'But you knew all along that he would leave most of his money to me, so it wasn't a surprise.'

235

'Yeh and you all think you are so clever. Well I'm the clever one here. He told me all about how Jet killed his father and how he was paying Jet so that Veronica didn't need to know how bad her precious son really was. Then he told me about David's treasure book and I knew that was my way out. I got Cecil to blackmail Charlie into leaving him the publishing house on the promise he wouldn't tell anyone about Jet. Then when Charlie died we got the manuscript and just had to wait until the pub was empty until we could get the treasure.'

'But you couldn't know Charlie would die before the manuscript was published.' Vicki said.

'Couldn't we?'

'Shut up Marisa, you silly cow,' Cecil shouted. 'They don't know anything and you don't need to tell 'em'

'You killed my dad?'

'Not tricky. He had a dodgy heart and more drugs in the house than a little. I just switched his heart drugs for some placebos, he'd brought home, I just had to wait for his heart to fail. It didn't take too long.'

'I can't believe you can stand there so calm, and tell me you killed my father.'

'Well it's my word against yours and I don't see how you are gonnna prove anything.'

'Unfortunately miss it doesn't work like that.' Out of the shadows appeared a tall rugged looking man in a beige trench coat. 'I'm Inspector Johnson, Ben's older brother.

He rang and suggested I could hide out down here tonight and see what developed. All right lads down you come,' he shouted up the cellar steps and four policemen appeared and immediately went to grab Baz and Trev. 'Not those two, idiots, those two,' he pointed at Cecil and Marisa.

As they were led back up the stairs, and out to the waiting patrol car, Inspector Johnson turned to David, Baz, Trev and Vicki. 'Well done guys. I had a tape recorder going but I think we will still need you to give evidence at the trial if that is okay?'

'No way.' Baz and Trev chorused in unison

'I will,' said Vicki tears running down her face still in shock.

'Me too,' said David.

'Well I suppose we could manage with just the two of you. Perhaps best not to mention that you two were down there,' he said looking at Baz and Trev.

'Thanks mate,' they chorused.

'Time for us to get out of here,' Baz said

'Time for you two to leave as well. I've got a lot of work

to carry out tonight and I don't need you in the way.'

'No problems and thanks for being here. I can't believe Mr Johnson didn't let us in on it.'

'I think he was more worried about Baz and Trev knocking the pub down, if they started a fight. No harm done. And I don't think you'd had been able to get so much information from her if you'd have know I was here. Anyway, off you go now and leave you details with the policeman at the door, so I can get hold of you for the trial.'

Chapter twenty three – Charlie's and a new start

Finally opening night of the club arrived. Jenny had been running round all week, finalising health and safety certificates, making sure she had plenty of people booked in to work and ensuring the night went well. The main party room was packed, with every table full and after the five course meal, the tables would be cleared to make way for a disco. The stage was set up and a comedian had been booked. The majority of people in the room were local office parties. Jenny hoped this would let all the locals see that the club was a meeting place as well as a strip club. The name had been changed and was tonight revealed as "Charlie's". As Vicki had walked up to the front door she had had to stop and look twice, it took a while to hold back the tears. How could her father have been such a good judge of character when it came to Jenny and such a bad judge of character when it had come to Marissa? The main room had a slight raised area at the back which was to become the VIP section but for tonight only, there was a very special table set up there for Jenny and her friends.

On the far left Mike sat smiling, thankful that everything had worked out okay. He had a job at the club and the money from Jenny had meant he could buy a small house out in the suburbs and start trying to live a normal life away from the club. Vicki had had a tough week and looked like she hadn't slept too well. She was wearing a stunning emerald green floor length gown and had her hair loose for a change. Blossom had been responsible for the ladies hair tonight and was thinking of offering her services full time. David sat next to Vicki and looked stunning in a tuxedo. Dilip look completely overwhelmed by everything that had happened in the last week. He had invited his finance, Jatinda. They were both dressed in traditional Indian outfits which meant they were wearing the brightest clothes in the club. Mindy and Blossom were sitting together and holding hands and smiling. Mindy dressed in a short nineteen fifties style prom dress with her hair in a pony tail and Blossom in a rather subdued, for her, black waist length wig and a long electric blue gown. Carly had decided on a tuxedo minus the shirt and with her figure it looked risqué but not slutty and then

Richard wore a traditional tuxedo and Jenny as the hostess wore a floor length one shouldered black gown with her hair tied in a lose ponytail and twisted down the shoulder without the material on it.
'Wow everything looks amazing.' Carly smiled at Jenny.
'Well it's taken a lot of work but I think it should all be worth it,' Jenny beamed.

240

'Of course it will darling. You know you have done everything that needs doing and look at the crowds. Once word gets around people are going to be queuing up to get into this place.' Richard said as he pulled her close and kissed her passionately on the lips. They had hardly been apart since the night at the spa and Jenny was enjoying every minute of it.

'Those two look happy,' Jenny said nodding at Mindy and Blossom.

'Yes I never realised,' Carly answered. 'They just wanted to see how it went before they let everyone know, but after everything that's happened, they thought it was time to be honest. Dilip and Jatinda have been round and Mindy said they've been great about

everything. She is going to try to talk to her mum but she doesn't know whether she cares if she accepts her and Blossom or not.'

'Well good for them.'

'And David it's nice to meet you at last,' Jenny shook his hand. 'I can believe you had the biggest adventure without me.'

'From what I hear you wouldn't have appreciated being called out of bed to come and join us,' Vicki chipped in.

'No she wouldn't, and nor would I,' called Richard over Jenny's head.

'So what happens for you now David?' Jenny smiled.

'Well the hole that Cecil discovered was an old passageway so people could escape from the castle before the pub was built. I don't think the gold is there but I am going ahead with publishing the book. We're going to try to make it more of an adventure and see if we can sell it as fiction.'

'So Vicki you're taking over the publishing house.'

'Yes I am. From what we can establish, Dad would have left it to me and no one else has any objections if I take it over. David is to be my first real client, although we are going to see if we can do anything with Mindy and Blossom's stories, especially now they have an ending together.'

'That sounds great.'

'And the other great news is we've solved the mystery of your and Blossoms attackers' Vicki said.

'What? When? How?' Jenny stuttered.

'Turns out Cecil was trying to keep you busy focusing on the buyout so you wouldn't look into what he was up to.'

'But that doesn't make sense, and why would he attack Blossom.'

'Apparently he knew Marissa from way back when, he had visited her in rehab once. He recognised Blossom from there and assumed she had recognised him.'

'But Blossom never said anything.'

'No. I spoke to her about in and she thinks it must have been not long after she first got there. She was in no fit state to remember anyone, but he obviously remembered her.'

'Looks like you won't need to protect me any more Richard,' Jenny smiled.

'I think I better stay close just in case.' Richard wrapped his arms round her.

'Where's Jet I thought he might join us?' Vicki asked. 'I haven't seen him for a while.'
'He would have loved to join us but unfortunately he starts work tonight so maybe next time.'
'What is he doing?'
'He's asked me not to say.'

'It's not dodgy is it? Mum will be so disappointed after everything you've done to get him on the straight and narrow.'

'No it's not dodgy but he wanted to tell you himself. I think he wants to check he enjoys it first before he explains it to you and his mum.'

'Anyway dinner's on its way so let's enjoy that and then

I show you round the club while it's full so you can enjoy it in its full glory.'

They all sat down to enjoy a fantastic Christmas style dinner. The starter was prawn cocktail, followed by turkey with all the trimmings, Christmas pudding, sorbet, cheeses and to finish coffee and mince pies. Considering the kitchen had just catered for two hundred people the turkey had been moist and not dry, the vegetables had been cooked but not over cooked and everyone seemed to have thoroughly enjoyed it.

Everyone was full after the dinner, that they all sat and enjoyed the comedian.

As the tables were being cleared to the side Jenny took to the stage.

'Good evening everyone, I hope you are all enjoying your evening so far,' a huge cheer when up around the room and Jenny couldn't help smiling. 'Now we are about to start the disco but as I am sure you are aware there are a number of speciality rooms either side of this, which you are welcome to go into, but please beware there will be nudity,' Yet another cheer mainly from the women in the room. 'So traditionally the men would go into the door on the left and the women into the room on the right, but we don't hold with tradition here, so go wherever you like or stay here and enjoy the disco. Whatever you decide to do I hope you enjoy your night and I look forward to seeing you here again soon.' The crowd cheered even louder still and Jenny passed the microphone back to the DJ so he could get the party started.

Jenny headed back to her friends and after they had enjoyed another drink they decided to see how the other rooms were doing. The disco was going well so they headed off into the room on the left and couldn't believe their eyes, it was empty.

'Oh well maybe the strip club is dead,' shrugged Jenny feeling a little disappointed.

'No I am sure it isn't. Most of the men out there are too scared to come in here whilst out with their work colleagues.' Carly offered some consolation.

'Okay well let's check the other room.'

They all walked across to the room where male strippers would perform and at first Jenny thought the door had been left locked. She couldn't believe they hadn't even opened the room. Then she realised someone was leaning against the door. She gave it a gentle but determined push and they managed to squeeze it to the room.

Much to Jenny's pleasure the room was absolutely

packed full of screaming women. The current stripper ripped his trousers off and stood with his back to the crowd showing off a pert bottom in a red lycra g-string. 'So the strip club isn't dead,' smiled Carly. 'Just different.'

Vicki then managed to squeeze in next to Jenny and Carly, 'I can believe how packed it is. These women are loving it and I can see why,' She smiled and nodded towards the wiggling bottom on the stage. At exactly that moment the stripper ripped off his g string and spun round to face the audience. He was beaming, quiet obviously loving every minute of his new found fame and the adoration of the crowd.

'Oh my god,' shouted Vicki above the screams of the

crowd. 'It's Jet.'

About the Author

Jo Jenner started writing professionally at the age of 40 and hasn't looked back since.

Jo still works as a certified accountant and manages to fit her writing in during evenings and weekends.

'Stripper of the Yard' is her first novel and started life during the 2012 National Novel Writing Month. NaNoWriMo is an annual competition where in excess of 300,000 people attempt to write a novel in just 30 days. Jo completed her first draft and took the following two years to develop and refine the story.

She enjoys writing short stories and a number of flash fiction stories have been published under the title of 'So the Feeling Shows'.

Always one for a challenge Jo took on the A to Z challenge in April 2014. This resulted in 'April Fool', which was written over 26 days in April, using a different letter of the alphabet for each chapter.

Jo lives with her husband on the south coast of England, her dream location, and says walks along the sea front always help generate story ideas.

If you enjoyed this why not post a review

Or check out Jo's other work

So the Feeling Shows and April Fool are both available on Amazon.

Jo can be found on Facebook

https://www.facebook.com/#!/jojennerauthor

Or twitter @jojenner40